Chocolate_Guitar_Momos

Kenny Deori Basumatary grew up with comics and books and practically never grew up beyond that. After performing well in academics throughout school in Guwahati, Tezpur and Lakhimpur in Assam, he did his best to undo all that damage by setting new records in low grade point averages during his four years at IIT Delhi. He outwitted the authorities there by getting out before they could kick him out. Three years as a news anchor at a regional satellite channel in Guwahati followed, after which a wise uncle said to him, 'If I were you I wouldn't be concerned about being comfortable. I'd go all out and fight to achieve my dreams.' The bulb lit up and Kenny finally made the move to Mumbai to work in the film industry as an actor and writer. In three years there, he has acted in six TV ads, Channel V's comedy show *Bollywood Nonsensex* and the online standup and sketch comedy show *Jay Hind!* He worked on the scripts of four films. One never got made, two almost got made, and one got made but hasn't been released. He has co-edited *75 Crazy People*, a 49-minute documentary on the making of the National Award-winning film *Frozen*. With his brother Tony, he has composed songs for and released *Brahmaputra*, an album of soft rock Assamese and Hindi songs which can be heard at http://soundclick.com/brahmaputra. Armed with a Canon 550D and his brother's audio studio, Kenny is presently working on his zero-budget action comedy feature, *Local Kung Fu*, where he fills all the minor crew positions of producer, director, writer, actor, composer, fight choreographer and the major crew positions of occasional make-up man, electrician, cook and driver.

Chocolate_Guitar_Momos is his first novel. Only one and a half chapters are true. The rest are all a pack of lies.

Chocolate_ Guitar_ Momos

Kenny Deori Basumatary

TRANQUEBAR

TRANQUEBAR PRESS
An imprint of westland ltd
Venkat Towers, 165, P.H. Road, Maduravoyal, Chennai 600 095
No. 38/10 (New No.5), Raghava Nagar, New Timber Yard Layout, Bangalore 560 026
Survey No. A-9, II Floor, Moula Ali Industrial Area, Moula Ali, Hyderabad 500 040
23/181, Anand Nagar, Nehru Road, Santacruz East, Mumbai 400 055
47, Briz Mohan Road, Daryaganj, New Delhi 110 002

First published by TRANQUEBAR PRESS, 2011

Copyright © Kenny Deori Basumatary, 2011

All Rights Reserved

10 9 8 7 6 5 4 3 2 1

ISBN: 978-93-80032-75-7

Typeset in Palatino Linotype by Mindways Design

Printed at Manipal Press Ltd.

This book is sold subject to the condition that it shall not by way of trade or otherwise, be lent, resold, hired out, circulated, and no reproduction in any form, in whole or in part (except for brief quotations in critical articles or reviews) may be made without written permission of the publishers.

Contents

1. Eight thousand, or, The Idiotic Notion of Still Remaining Friends — 1
2. Seven thousand, or, The Addition of Additional Insult to Insult Previously Added to Injury — 14
3. Haystack Needles are Easier — 26
4. Into the Drain — 47
5. A Year Goes By — 56
6. The Minor Benefits of Not Getting Seduced Too Easily — 57
7. Look Left, Look Right, Look Left Again, then Cross—If there are no Vehicles — 76
8. Soulmates and Sole Mates — 80
9. The Exciting Wedding Video — 83
10. Soulmates & Sole Mates—II — 91
11. Don't think of Elephants — 103
12. Swallowing Pride and Dough — 113
13. Freezing Fingers & More — 121
14. Words that Draw Attention in Coffee Shops — 134

15. Going to Shillong	144
16. Role Reversal	164
17. Debuting In a New Field of Enterprise	175
18. Hyperactive Imagination	190
19. Making Memories	224
20. The End	236
21. Flashback to a Year Now Gone	237
22. Four Months Later	242

Chapter 1

Eight thousand, or, The Idiotic Notion of Still Remaining Friends

The terrible, bludgeoning, grating, forcefully ominous saas-bahu background music emanating from the TV in Moon Internet Café should have been ample warning for Joseph. However, he was in a good mood, having finished recording and mixing the self-composed anniversary song which he was now going to email to his beloved.

As he waited for the mp3 to get attacked—sorry, attached—Joseph wondered whether Moon, the café owner, was disciplining himself into a state of advanced retardation by watching serials where one line of dialogue was followed by 35 flash pans and 40 flash zoom-ins of 57 relatives' faces accompanied by the crashing of 68 cymbals.

Joseph clicked on the send button and then called Uma.

'Yeah?' answered her sleepy and not-too-enthusiastic voice.

'You awake, darling?'

'Sort of.'

'Well then, happy fifth anniversary!'

'Yeah.'

'Is everything all right? Or are you just sleepy?'

'I'm fine.'

'I've just mailed you my gift. It's a new song. For a change, I've tried to sing it myself. It'll be a little besura at places, but I wanted to make it really personal this time.'

'Joseph, we need to talk.'

Joseph had read somewhere that 'We need to talk' = 'I need to complain.' With Uma, this definitely was the case. The subject needed to be talked about was invariably never about how good last night's boiled chicken was. Joseph's brain went into quick-rewind-and-play mode to try and figure out what he could possibly have done wrong over the 1959-km distance, she being in Delhi and he in Guwahati. Nothing suggested itself.

'What's the matter?' he said.

'I think we need to take a break for a while.'

'A break? What break?'

'I mean a break from this relationship.'

Only at this moment did Joseph notice the appropriateness of the foreboding saas-bahu music, which was adding a natural discordant background score to the mood of the moment.

'Why?' he said, genuinely puzzled.

'I don't think I can wait any longer for you.'

'But—but it hasn't even been a year.'

'Okay, less than a year since you've been back in Guwahati, but what about the year you spent hanging around here trying scrape together` a non-existent music career? You didn't finish your PG here—just wasted your time with those useless wannabe rock stars.'

'We'd have reached somewhere if Ritu hadn't quit.'

'At least he had the sense to know what to quit. You quit your studies and stuck with your music. And now your so-called music career is going nowhere back home either. So what d'you expect me to do?'

'You could give me some time.'

'Five years is a lot of time.'

'Look, it's been less than a year—in fact just about eight months—since I started out seriously as a musician. It's tough. I'm a newbie nobody and everyone's always trying to get work done for free or for peanuts.'

'That's not my fault. You already knew that when you went back, didn't you?'

'Things are changing slowly.'

'Like hell they are. You should've gone to Bombay, where all the music action actually is, but no, you just had to go back to the safety of home and lusi-bhaji and pork momos.'

Joseph was stunned by the low blow.

'That's a low blow.'

'Whatever.'

The getting-dumped version of adrenaline kicked in and Joseph processed the whole situation in a flash. There could be only one explanation for this...

'You—you've found someone else?' he said slowly.

'... No.'

'Don't lie. I know that tone.'

'Okay, yes.'

On TV, cymbals crashed to underline some Tauji's dialogue so that even the most moronic person watching would understand that something of importance had transpired. The cymbals felt amplified to Joseph's ears.

'Who?'

'Someone you know.'

More cymbals crashed.

'Who the hell?'

'Tonmoy.'

'What!'

Cymbals! Trumpets! Strings! Flash zooms! Flash pans!

Joseph's head began spinning. The only time he had previously felt this sensation was when playing football once in his college hostel, when the ball had come down from miles high and he had dived upwards to use his head to send it back up again. He had defied gravity by about one measly foot, whereas the ball had on its side at least sixty feet of accumulated gravity, which unloaded itself on Joseph's skull with such a resounding bonk that he was promptly rendered horizontal.

At the present moment, it felt like his skull was in one place, but his brain was making slow revolutions around it in an orbit about one and a half feet in radius.

'How—what—how did this happen?' he blurted.

'Remember the trip to Manali I told you about?'

'And—?'

'We were there together for two full days. When we left, he kissed me goodbye... on the lips.'

Joseph was hearing everything, but it seemed like someone was telling him a story about someone else, not about him and his girlfriend.

'What a humungous, backstabbing fart! He took your number from me and now he's trying to take you from me?... What happened next?'

'Do you really want all the gory details?'

'Gory details? There are actually gory details?... Tell me. Tell me all the gory details!'

'When we got back, he came to see me at my place after a couple of days... and we... sort of made out.'

Two days! She met a guy for two days and it blew away the previous five years! Joseph wasn't yet voicing these thoughts. He wanted to hear the story first, out of the same morbid curiosity which leads people to watch *sansani* crime programmes on news channels where the anchor yells at the audience as if he's accusing *them* of being the murderer/cheat/etc.

'You made out with clothes on or off?' Joseph asked slowly.

There was a pause.

'You did it, didn't you?' he said. He was surprised at the calm in his voice. Barring a wee tremor, there was hardly any sign of his inner turmoil.

'Yes,' she said, sounding only a little guilty.

'And how was it?'

'Better than you,' she said after a pause.

Joseph couldn't find anything to say. In fact, he didn't want to say anything. He still loved her, but all that weight she'd put on had been puncturing his libido. Yet, he'd remained faithful to her, despite having received the seductive attentions of at least three girls in the last five years.

'I'm sorry, Joseph, but I think it's time for a change. It's time we moved on.'

'You—think it's so easy?' Joseph croaked.

'I know it's not. Breaking up is always hard, but your life really doesn't seem to be going anywhere.'

Joseph let this sink in. She was right, wasn't she? His life indeed wasn't going anywhere.

'Is that your main reason?'

'No, the main reason is I've fallen in love with Tonmoy.'

'In two days?' said Joseph, laying emphasis on the 'two'.

'Love can happen very fast.'

Love? Blast love! This wasn't love. It was lust. It was understandable lust—the ill-fated, illegitimate child of an eight-month separation of two young bodies that longed for each other.

'In two days?'

'It's been more than a month now.'

'A month! This guy's been with you for a month now!'

'Face it, Joseph. This is life. You have to move on. I already have.'

As if on cue, Tonmoy, who had been sleeping in Uma's bed all along, sat up and gave her a hug, saying, 'Morning baby.'

The words carried over the airwaves to Joseph's ears. 'That's him, isn't it? Give him the phone.'

'What for?' said Uma. 'You'll just shout and create an unnecessary situation. I'm in no mood for drama.'

Joseph gnashed his teeth and said, 'I'm. Not. Going. To. Shout. I can handle these things in a mature manner.'

At the other end, Uma held the phone out to Tonmoy. Who, said his quizzical eyebrows. Just take it, said Uma's impatient scowl. Tonmoy saw Joseph's name and oh no, said his sigh.

'Hello, Joseph.'

'You backstabbing asshole sonofabitch snake-in-the-grass asshole!' yelled Joseph.

'You've said "asshole" twice,' said Tonmoy, almost disinterested.

'I'll say "asshole" as many times as I like, asshole!'

Uma said, 'I can hear you shouting.'

Moon, the internet café owner, whose intense, concentrated viewing of the saas-bahu drama was being interrupted by Joseph's real-life drama, said, 'Oi! Go outside if you want to shout.'

Joseph stepped outside and continued his civilised conversation.

'Was this always the plan, you @#$*& asshole!' he shouted. 'To sneak up behind my back and steal my girlfriend from me when I wasn't looking? I give you her number so she could help you make some contacts and this is how you return the favour! By making contact with her! You @#$%*& stinking snake!'

'Hey look,' said Tonmoy.

'I can't "look" over the phone, you moron!'

'Okay, fine. Then listen. I found that she was sad and lonely, I tried to make her happy and give her some company, and one thing led to another. We couldn't help it. These things aren't in our control, so just calm down.'

'I'll calm down after I've murdered you and danced on your ashes, you twofaced shitbrained asshole bastard!'

Tonmoy scoffed in disbelief. That set Joseph off even more.

'What! Are you actually finding this funny, you gigantic fart of poison gas!'

Uma snatched the phone back from Tonmoy and said to Joseph, 'Real mature, eh?'

Joseph tried to regain his cool. 'What, Uma, babe—what did you see in him—of all people?'

'At least he's got a successful career.'

'He's just a brown-nosing arse-licking corporate slave.'

'Whatever! At least he can afford to take me to decent restaurants.'

Joseph felt a sock in the gut. No sensitivity. No softening the blows. No diplomacy. No slowly breaking the bad news. Just one brutal gash after another.

'You can still call me, you know,' said Uma. 'We can be friends. I can help you get through this.'

Joseph felt like he'd just been shot and the assassin was now recommending a good undertaker and just the right cemetery. He thought of asking Uma whether she'd taken a crash course called How To Maintain A Break-up Helpline, but then decided that sarcasm would not get him very far in the current situation. He tried a more pragmatic tone.

'Listen, baby, I'm sure this is just a passing phase. You've been missing me too much, this fartface came and seduced you, but deep down inside I'm sure that we still love each other. Let's just cool down and talk.

Everything will be all right again once we meet. I'll come over next month. We can forget about all this. Put it behind us.'

'I won't be here. Tonmoy's helping me move to Bombay.'

Goodbye to the pragmatic tone. 'What! He's taken you and he's taking you away as well!'

'What's that even supposed to mean?'

'When are you going?'

'Next week.'

'Next week? Next week! Everything's turned upside down so quickly?'

Uma didn't reply.

'What about my bike?' said Joseph. He'd intended to bring it to Guwahati on his next trip.

'I sold it off.'

'You what?'

'I sold it off.'

'You sold off my bike! Without so much as telling me? Forget about asking.'

'It nearly got stolen twice.'

'So? And what d'you mean nearly got stolen? Did you personally chase the thieves away when they were smack in the middle of carrying it off? What?'

'I emailed you about it.'

'I didn't get no mail about this.'

'Well, it probably didn't get delivered.'

Joseph felt his intestines go into convulsions. With great effort, he restrained himself and said, 'This is *email* you're talking about. It's not the Indian postal service that the mail could get lost along the way.'

'Whatever.'

'Why? Why did you do it? This was Tonmoy's idea?'

'I need the money to move. I'll pay you back within three months.'

'How much did you sell it for?'

'Eight thousand.'

Joseph couldn't believe his ears. He wouldn't have been able to believe someone else's ears either.

'Eight—eight thousand,' he said, struggling to come to grips with the amount. 'You sold off a bike in tip-top condition for eight thousand measly bucks? When it could have fetched at least twenty to twenty-five.'

'I was in a hurry.'

'Thieves usually are.' Joseph had crossed the line from anguish to anger. 'Are you lying about selling it for only eight thousand or were you really stupid enough to settle for that little?'

'I was stupid! Stupid to ever stick with you!' said Uma, and cut the call.

'Hello—dammit!'

Joseph tried calling her again only to hear an extremely irritating woman's voice informing him that the number he was trying was currently switched off.

He cut the call and looked around, in a daze. The sun was shining. A few birds were happily chirping.

Schoolgirls were tittering. An unseen someone with a guitar was playing Marty Friedman's *Tibet*. Everything was perfect for a fifth anniversary. Except for the natural disaster that had just unloaded itself on him.

Shit. I've been dumped, he said to himself.

He staggered towards the bus stop.

Shit. I've been dumped.

He sat down on the concrete seat.

Shit. I've been dumped.

Bus number 3 came by. Joseph usually avoided it like the plague because it was the stinkiest bus of all, but on this occasion, he didn't notice. He climbed aboard and plonked down on a seat beside a woman whose mouth reeked of various combinations of betel nuts and leaves and tobacco.

'Bhai, time kiman?' the woman said to him.

Joseph wasn't part of this world. He looked at her with unseeing eyes, then muttered:

'Shit. I've been dumped.'

'Ki?' said the woman in utter incomprehension.

Joseph didn't reply. He turned away, then said to himself:

'Shit. I've been bloody dumped.'

The woman looked at Joseph, then turned her face towards the window, muttering, 'Paagol.'

Joseph's phone rang. It was Uma. He hurriedly pressed the green button.

'Hello?'

'Listen,' said Uma, 'remember the 2,300 bucks you'd borrowed from me the last time?'

'Yeah?'

'Never mind the 300. I'll be deducting 2,000 from the amount I give you.'

Joseph was too numb to react to this offer of a break-up discount on a personal loan. Addition of insult to injury was too light a term. Up until then, he had been the victim of a break-up. That was par for the course. But this—this was something even the spirit of Shylock would have smiled and nodded at in approval.

Joseph's eloquent response was 'Hm.'

'Okay, bye then... We can still be friends, you know.'

Joseph couldn't find an appropriate rejoinder. He simply cut the call.

Shit. I've been dumped. And shat upon.

CHAPTER 2

Seven thousand, or, The Addition of Additional Insult to Insult Previously Added to Injury

THERE ARE TWO TYPES OF METHODOLOGIES FOR DEALING with break-ups. Broadly speaking, one is passive and the other is active. The passive mode is preferred by whiny, self-pitying, life-sucks-complaining, why-me type of individuals. In short, the Devdas type. This category of dumped lovers usually takes to the bottle for a few weeks at least, all the while listening to the most tragic dukhi-aatma broken-heart Rafi-ke-dukh-bhare-naghme kind of songs. Because of this, Joseph suspected that every bus, truck and auto driver in the country was in a state of continuous break-up, and that their revelling in this negative state of self-pity was part of the reason why they weren't rising above their present station in life.

On the other hand, dealing with a break-up is an acquired skill for the other category of heartbroken lovers, who usually take concrete steps to get over break-ups.

Joseph bravely tried to keep himself in the latter category. He put all the photos he had of Uma in a packet and stuffed it into a deep corner of a cupboard. He had recently bought a CD of Nepali ballads by Adrian Pradhan, but decided not to listen to them until much later because they were all tragic, although beautiful, and might just contribute to a rise in any possible suicidal tendencies. Of course, he wasn't the type to do any such thing, but he would rather not actively do anything to worsen his state of mind either.

He became a bit of a recluse, devoting most of his time to practising guitar and trying to get his voice to stay in key. Unfortunately, most of his favourite songs only served to make him cry. But he consoled himself, saying that one needed to hit rock bottom to bounce back up.

Utpal, his long-time friend and present housemate, did his best to see his buddy through, by doing the sensible thing of not delivering any 'inspirational' speeches or lectures. He just let him be. It helped that Utpal himself didn't have a girlfriend, so Joseph was spared the painful sight of a close friend coochie-cooing with a loved one.

On one of the few occasions that Utpal alluded to Joseph's state-of-the-heart matters, he said, 'The more the break-ups, the easier they get to handle. The first break-up takes three months to get over, the second six weeks, and the third one eight days.'

'Why eight days?' said Joseph. 'Why not nine?'

'Research says so.'

'Really? Whose research?'

'Mine.'

Joseph gave Utpal a wordless look. Mistaking it for a cue to continue, Utpal said, 'On the other hand, if you meet a new girl soon, then recovery is quick. Recovery period is inversely proportional to the hotness of the new girl multiplied by the number of days before you first do it with her. But you can't do the deed without some level of emotional investment. Which is why hookers don't count. Not even the golden-hearted Chandramukhi types.'

'Have you ever met a golden-hearted Chandramukhi-type hooker?'

'Good lord, no. What d'you think I am?'

'You mean you're the type who only goes to black-hearted hookers?'

'No, mokkel. I'm the type who doesn't go to hookers at all.'

'I don't get it. I just don't. I don't dump anybody. Why does everyone always dump me? It's not fair. If I'd dumped at least two-three girls I'd have understood it's karma, but I've always been loyal and good to everyone.'

'Why did Prarthana dump you?'

'She said she wouldn't be able to marry a non-Hindu.'

'And who is she married to now?'

'Amanpreet Singh Gulati.'

'What about Madhusmriti?'

'She said she wanted someone with a stable career, not a future musician.'

'Hm… Basically, she meant she wanted to marry some moneybags. Where's she now?'

'Delhi. Married to a bloke fifteen years older.'

'Tsk tsk. Were all the young men dead?'

'The guy owns two petrol pumps.'

'Well, may someone throw a burning cigarette butt in his petrol pumps while he's busy counting the day's cash.'

Two months went by and the pain hadn't yet eased to any comfortable level. Joseph decided that hitting rock bottom was now absolutely essential to recovery. So he stopped shaving and started listening to every tragic song he could lay his hands on, in the hope that he would get bored of the whole thing one fine day and say to himself, 'What the hell's wrong with you? Stop moaning and move on!' The one thing that he couldn't do was to stop eating regularly. No matter how serious or how tragic a situation was, Joseph just could not function without food.

As they walked home one evening, Utpal said to him, 'Dude, I think it's time you dropped the Dev D look.'

'Any particular reason?'

'Naba's birthday party is coming up. You're not gonna attract any new girlfriends with this weird beard.'

'What's wrong with it?'

'Well, nothing's wrong. But nothing's right either. It's just not dense enough to look sexy. And we're still too young for beards. They look perfect on people like Shekhar Kapur and Captain Haddock.'

Joseph tried to catch a glimpse of himself in a shop window.

'It's okay to grieve,' said Utpal. 'In fact, you've done a pretty commendable job of it. Two weeks, three weeks, four weeks, fine. But it's been two months now. I think it's enough. Time to move on. Do something new. Remove the facial jungle. Do something drastic. Get yourself a bike.'

'That reminds me,' said Joseph. He took out his cell and called Uma.

'Hello?' she said. To Joseph, the tone sounded like she thought he was a tele-salesman trying to sell a magic weight-loss machine, which, incidentally, he felt she was in dire need of.

'Uma, hi. It's been two months now and I've been thinking of getting myself a bike. So…'

'Yeah. Remember you owe me two thousand?'

'Yes I do.'

'And remember I also bought you those shoes?'

Joseph looked down. They were the very shoes he was wearing. 'Yeah?'

'Minus 2,500 for those too.'

Joseph wanted to say, 'What the @#$*!' but he simply uttered a very loaded 'Okay?' in the same tone.

'That leaves 2,500.'

'3,500,' corrected Joseph.

'No, no. 7,000 minus 2,000 minus 2,500.'

'Seven? You said you got eight thousand for the bike.'

'It was seven.'

This was crossing over into the absurdly funny.

'Why're you being so cheap?' said Joseph, almost chuckling in disbelief. 'You'd said eight thousand.'

'I never said eight. It was seven. And I owe you 2,500. Take it or leave it.'

This was the last straw.

'I'm leaving it, you cheap bitch! You can keep it all. I'd rather be able to tell people you're a bike thief than take your charity scraps! Piss off!'

Joseph wished that like in the days before cell phones, he could slam down the receiver, but that wasn't a possibility any more, so he just pressed the end call key in as exaggerated a manner as possible.

Utpal asked him, totally deadpan, 'So is she returning the money?'

'I don't believe this,' said Joseph, almost laughing. 'What a cheap bitch. What an absolutely cheap bitch.'

'What was all that seven thousand eight thousand stuff?'

Joseph looked at his shoes. The shoes she had gifted him. And he snapped. He violently yanked them off and headed for the nearby Jonali culvert, beneath which ran a large drain whose chief function was to overflow during the monsoon.

'What're you doing?' said Utpal.

Standing in just his socks, Joseph lifted the shoes like a baseball pitcher about to pitch, aiming for the drain.

'What the hell are you doing? Don't! Give them to someone if you don't want 'em, but don't waste things like this.'

'I'll burn them.'

'Like hell. Give them to Daaju's boy.'

Daaju's nameless little restaurant was the place where they frequently had breakfast—parathas, pulao, lusi-bhaji et al. Without a word, Joseph dropped the idea of shot-putting the shoes and set off towards Daaju's.

The young boy who assisted him was too delighted with the shoes to ask why Joseph was being so charitable. When Daaju asked, Utpal said, 'They're too tight for him.'

Joseph walked the rest of the way home in just socks. People stared.

'Maybe I should keep a distance,' said Utpal. 'I have a reputation.'

In the ice-cream-cum-photostat shop opposite the Rajgarh Bihutoli, they saw an obviously-in-love young couple sharing an ice-cream cone.

Joseph muttered, 'She'll dump him next week.'

Later that evening, Utpal returned from the pork shop and was surprised to find Joseph sitting and staring at a quarter bottle of whisky on his table.

'What da health is this?' said Utpal. 'I thought I told you to end the Dev D phase, not start the post-interval section.'

Everyone in Joseph's family boozed. Except for him. His parents had let him try out everything as a kid, believing that non-forbidden fruit wouldn't be too attractive. The idea worked, too, and so while all of Joseph's friends, at least the ones left in Guwahati, always looked for an excuse to drink, he himself looked upon alcohol as a resort of the weak. The only thing he drank, that too at most a glass of, was traditional rice wine.

'Asshole,' said Utpal, 'you used to tell me to drink only in happy times, not in times of tragedy, and you're yourself doing that now.'

As Joseph poured himself his first peg, he said, 'Being a good guy doesn't count anymore. Only the notes you can count in your bank account count.'

'Dude, practise what you preach! You said it's dangerous to drink in bad times.'

'Did I? Well, you can tell me from me that I'm a total nincompoop.'

And with that, Joseph took his first sip. A long one. He grimaced and said, 'Bloody horse piss! Why da health do people drink?'

'Now you listen to me,' said Utpal. He picked up the bottle and started pouring the whisky out of the window.

'What're you doing?'

'Shut up. You can have that one peg just to remind you that it tastes like shit.'

'Piss.'

'Whatever. My point is, you've got a lot of qualities in you. Talent, honesty, ambition. My folks always used to tell me to be like you. So I wised up and got serious. Whereas *you* started screwing up your life.'

As Utpal's long-overdue discourse continued, the whisky was taking a short little trip of its own. The two of them lived on the first floor, and beneath the window was a shed with a tin roof. Beside the shed were rose bushes. Attending to those rose bushes was the landlord, Mr Dharanidhar Dhar. And it was on his almost-bald head that the whisky was falling, in the process also wetting his full-sleeved banian and pyjamas.

Mr Dharanidhar Dhar sniffed. He stood up. The whisky started falling on a rose bush.

Back in their room, Utpal was concluding his dressing-down of Joseph. 'You might want to turn into a drunk loser like many of our good-for-nothing-anymore buddies, but I don't *want* you to turn into a drunk loser. *Understand?!'*

The ferocity of the last word pretty much startled Joseph. He managed a nod, suddenly not in much of a mood for horse piss anymore.

'I'll be honest with you now, because I think this has gone far enough,' said Utpal. 'I'm really, really glad that Uma dumped you. She was a humungous bitch. And you knew it too.'

'Why didn't you tell me back then?'

'Love is blind. You think a fool in love can see any of his darling's faults? She could well be a kleptomaniac and the guy would still love her.'

'Uma *was* a bit of a kleptomaniac.'

'What!'

'Well, not exactly a kleptomaniac. But she liked to steal things from shops. Cassettes, earrings, soft toys.'

Utpal was at a loss for words.

'There was one occasion when she wanted me to distract some footpath chap selling girls' tops while she filched one at the other end. The blokes sensed it, though. They kept an eye on her and she couldn't steal anything. Later she blamed me for it and made me the butt of jokes.'

'I don't know what to say. This is the girl you stuck with? I'm no longer surprised she sold off your bike. It had to happen. What kind of moron were you?'

'A rare kind.'

'Never mind,' said Utpal as he picked up Joseph's acoustic guitar. 'You know what you should do now?'

Playing the end chords of the Eagles song, he loudly sang, 'Get over it! Get over it! Get over it!'

Ding dong! The doorbell. It was Utpal's turn to have a mini heart attack.

Joseph opened the door.

'Oh, hi, Uncle.'

'Hello Joseph,' said Mr Dhar with a smile.

'You're drenched. Is it raining?'

'Believe it or not, it's raining whisky.'

'Oops,' mouthed Utpal to himself.

Mr Dhar pleasantly said, 'Next time you don't feel like drinking any more, just give me the bottle.'

'Yes, Uncle, we will. Very very sorry about this.'

'Sorry, Uncle,' said Utpal. 'My fault.'

'That's all right. But wasting good whisky isn't all right, eh? Heh heh heh...'

Mr Dhar wasn't all up there, but he was definitely the ideal landlord. He cast them a partners-in-crime smile and left.

'Idiot,' said Joseph to Utpal as he shut the door.

'How was I to know he'd position himself right under the whisky falls?'

Joseph walked up to the table, took a look at his glass, picked it up and emptied it into the sink.

'Good boy,' said Utpal.

'Tomorrow, I'm making a fresh start.'

'Very good. I know what we should do: exercise. I've been procrastinating for far too long. We'll wake up early and go jogging. Nothing like exercise to release some feel-good hormones.'

Chapter 3

Haystack Needles are Easier

'Wake up, mokkel!' said Joseph as he tried to shake Utpal awake. Utpal's alarm had already gone off thrice.

Utpal forced his eyelids open and saw that Joseph had rid himself of the wannabe beard. 'Who're you and how did you get in?' he mumbled.

Twenty minutes later, they were on the Chandmari flyover. The sun was already up, but Utpal wasn't fully. They paused to catch their breath in the middle of the flyover. The view from here early in the morning was always soothing. There was something serene, almost poetic, about the sun rising right over GNB Road, one of the arterial roads of the city, as though it was lighting up the road to better things.

'Okay, that does it,' said Joseph. 'Enough of messing around. I'm going to find my soulmate.'

'They live in Shillong.'

Utpal's extremely poor joke was a reference to the blues band Soulmate.

'I'm surprised you can come up with such a shitty joke so early in the morning,' said Joseph. 'But at least it shows you're alive and well.'

'What soulmate?'

'I've never told you about that girl, have I?'

'You have.'

'Which girl?'

'I don't know.'

'Cut the crap and come on. I'll show you where it happened.'

As they walked towards Zoo Road Tiniali, Joseph said, 'It was eight years ago.'

'A dark night,' said Utpal. 'Rainy and stormy. There was a girl in a white dress standing in the middle of the road.'

'Shuddup. It was nothing of the kind. It was a sunny morning in 2002.'

Pointing to the corner where Zoo-Narengi Road started, Joseph said, 'I was about to cross the road to get to the bus stop, and there she was crossing from the bus stop to this side. The important thing to remember here is that she wasn't the drop-dead gorgeous kind; not the type a producer sees and immediately approaches to act in his next film. She was average-looking, I guess. I don't remember the facts, just the impressions.'

'I'm impressed,' said Utpal, taking in the location and trying to visualise a black and white or sepia-toned flashback.

'Shuddup. Where was I? Yeah. I looked at her. She looked right back at me. Our eyes met, and get this—we smiled at each other. I couldn't help it; the smile just forced its way out. And I think it was the same for her, because she cast a shy sort of aside glance for an instant before looking at me again. Still smiling. Her expression was "Why am I smiling at this guy?"'

"Because I'm stoned?" offered Utpal.

'Shuddup. I still can't explain it. It was just a pleasant feeling that came from somewhere deep within.'

'More likely from somewhere down below.'

'Piss off. She wasn't the type of girl you see and go "Ssss—I want that ass." It was a spiritual connection.'

'Okay. So what happened next? Did you get the number of her phone connection as well?'

'No.'

'No? Why?'

'I was with Madhu at the time.'

Utpal slapped his forehead. 'So you just let that girl go?'

'Yeah.'

'You didn't even say hi?'

'No.'

'So that means you don't know her name?'

'No.'

'What kind of maha mokkel are you? You expected school-college romances to last forever? You should've taken her name and number and permanent residential address and told her you'd get in touch if ever you were both single again. Wait a minute... The whole point of your fairy tale is—this is the girl you wanna find?'

Joseph nodded.

'You don't know her name or number?'

Joseph shook his head.

'Her email id?'

Joseph rolled his eyes.

'I hope you at least remember what she looks like.'

Joseph smiled a slow, wide smile.

'What is that asinine, doped-out smile supposed to mean?'

'I don't remember.'

'You don't remember? This is your supposed dream girl and you don't even remember her face?'

'It was eight years ago.'

'Well, obviously she can't have been "the one" if you don't even remember what she looks like.'

'I told you, I don't remember the facts and the faces, just the impressions.'

'Ridd-diculous.'

'Why haven't I forgotten that incident even after all these years? That whole encounter lasted less than a minute. Can you give me one good reason why I should remember it for eight years running now?'

'You have a good memory.'

'If that were the case, I'd remember her face as well, wouldn't I?'

'I suddenly feel hungry. Let's grab a bite.'

They entered Rookman restaurant and ordered parathas. While the parathas there were good, the chutney was the USP of the place.

'Look,' said Joseph as they ate, 'I know it's weird, but I seriously think that that girl was my soulmate, and on that day, whoever is up there pulling all the strings, had given me my once-in-a-lifetime chance to hook up with her, but I, dunderhead that I was, missed it.'

'Dude, eight years have whizzed by. Right now she's probably spanking the shit out of one kid and breastfeeding another.'

'Y'know what—this is my last gamble. If all that lifetime love crap they sing about in songs is even a little bit true, then maybe that girl's still around somewhere. Maybe I still have a chance. All I have to do is find her.'

'Without name, address, nothing. If you at least remembered her face we could've gotten some police sketch artist to draw her and put up "Wanted: Dead or Alive" posters.'

Joseph smiled.

'What's that sneaky smile for?' Utpal asked.

'There's one definite detail I do remember.'

'What? A front tooth was missing? Her bra strap was purple?'

'She was wearing a grey skirt.'

Utpal paused for a moment and tried to wash this bit of information down with a spoon of ghugni. 'Oh. So my purple bra strap wasn't very far off the mark. Grey skirt, eh? So what do we do? Put an ad out in the papers? "All girls wearing a grey skirt at the Tiniali bus stop one morning in 2002 report to Joseph". Quickly. Before they get married."

'Think like Sherlock Holmes. All we have to do is search among the girls who were in 2002 in those junior colleges which had grey skirt uniforms.'

'Faculty, Maria's, Vidya Mandir, Swadeshi,' said Utpal as he paid the bill.

'That's right. Can't be too many of them.'

'So your plan is to go to all these colleges and ask for names, photos and addresses of all their female students in 2002?'

'Maybe.'

Utpal smiled and put a condescending arm around Joseph as they walked out of the restaurant.

'Look, buddy, you've taken this break-up too hard. It's affected your brain and your faculties. I thought you were almost over it, but I see there's still a few steps to go. No one is going to give you that information. The only addresses you'll be sent to are Chandmari police station from Vidya Mandir, Geetanagar police station from Maria's and Faculty, and Paltan Bazar police station from Swadeshi. Let's just have you meet girls the normal way—common friends, parties, weddings.'

Joseph mulled over this for a moment, then said, 'You know that speech they give—think of your life twenty, thirty years down the line. What if I don't try to find this girl and I'm stuck with some other girl who's not fully compatible with me and I with her? I don't want to have the regret that I didn't even try to track down the one girl I felt that divine, ethereal, whatever, connection with. I don't want to spend my life thinking "I wish I'd at least tried to find her."'

'Okay. What if you do find her and she's got six kids?'

'This whole idea is based on the hopelessly romantic notion that there's a special someone for everyone. If it's true, then I'm sure she'll still be available, one way or another.'

'Whoa. What does that mean—one way or another?'

'And one more thing. My gut feeling tells me—she'll turn out to be a great singer. We'll be a made-for-each-other match.'

'Oh God! This guy wants to have his cake, eat it too, and then do an *American Pie* with it.'

Joseph decided that the school and college authorities would surely fling him out on his arse if he went asking for rosters of female students, nor was he silly enough to hire a policeman's uniform and say he needed the information for a slander case. His waist was too slim to make a convincing policeman.

Between him and Utpal, they both had friends who had studied at all the aforementioned junior colleges in the critical year. Joseph's plan was to peruse class and other photos, believing that the face of his bus stop girl would somehow leap out at him.

He commenced his search with Parul's photos of her days at Faculty Higher Secondary School.

'Are you crazy?' she said.

'I thought you already knew,' said Utpal.

'Let me try at least. It might just work,' said Joseph.

'Yeah, let him try. If nothing, it'll at least distract him from tragic thoughts of Paro—I mean Uma.'

Parul brought out four thick photo albums and handed them to Joseph.

'I must say, though,' she said, 'I'm glad she dumped you. She was a bit of a bitch.'

'Fat lot of good it's going to do, telling me now. Why didn't you warn me back then?'

'It's not the kind of thing you tell a guy blindly in love. Besides, there's an obvious conflict of interest.' Parul's sister had had a long crush on Joseph.

'Hm... you're starting to sound like a liar already—I mean a lawyer.'

The four albums were neatly divided into photos of Parul's times at Holy Child School, Faculty, Cotton College and J B Law College.

Joseph took a long hard look at the girls' faces in a Faculty class photo.

'Is that her?' said Utpal, pointing at a random girl.

'Cute, but I don't think so,' said Joseph.

'I'm curious—why is it that you don't remember anything about her except the grey skirt?' said Parul.

'And what if she was a school girl?' said Utpal. 'St Mary's alone will have a thousand or two girls in grey skirts.'

'There are two things I can say about her with certainty,' said Joseph. 'One is the grey skirt and the other her age. The reason I remember the skirt is this: after she was out of sight, the exact thought I had in my mind was, "If I ever have to find her again, I'll need to remember that she was wearing a grey skirt."'

'Ohhhhhhh,' said Parul.

'How very far-sighted,' said Utpal.

'What about her age?'

'Well, I guess you could call it a little specialty of mine. Estimating people's ages. I'm not too accurate with people over sixty, but up until then, I'm rarely off by more than a year or two.'

'And where did you do your PhD in this?' asked Parul.

'I suppose it started from wanting to be Sherlock Holmes—guessing people's occupations from the dent in their front tooth—that sort of thing. I was crap at that, but I got good at looking for the right indicators of age.'

'Such as?'

'Necklines.'

'Eh?'

'I mean neck lines. Lines on the neck. And crow's feet. And best of all—the back of the hand. People may apply tons of anti-wrinkle creams and moisturisers and what not, but the skin on the back of the hand tells the truest story.'

Both Utpal and Parul looked at the backs of their hands.

'How old am I?' said Parul.

'Twenty-six?'

'Wow,' said Parul in mock awe. 'How did you guess? Because we were in the same class?'

'Somebody kill me,' said Utpal.

'Anyway, the point is, I had also made a mental note: she must be exactly my age.'

'It's still too thin for me,' said Parul. 'But even assuming that she is our age, how the hell are you going to find her? There must have been hundreds of grey-skirted girls that year.'

Joseph was to repeat this explanation a dozen times over the next couple of months.

'She would have been either Higher Secondary 1st year or 2nd year. Now, roughly assuming that Faculty had one section for science and two for arts with approximately fifty students each, half of whom were girls, that would make it twenty-five students per class multiplied by three sections multiplied by two batches, so that makes it 150 girls. We make similar calculations for the other junior colleges and we'll probably end up with around 400-500 girls.'

'You're going to interview all of them?'

'That won't be necessary. We'll eliminate the tall ones, the short ones, the fat ones, the walking matchsticks, the ghostly white types, the very dark ones—which is a pity, because I have a thing for very dark skin—the supermodel types, and the aesthetically very challenged ones. That should leave us 250-300 girls to investigate.'

'You're crazy,' said Parul.

'What do you mean "investigate"?' said Utpal. 'And more importantly, what d'you mean "we"?'

Joseph ignored Utpal and flipped through a few more photos. Pointing at one, he asked, 'Who's this?'

'Rajeshwari. Married now. In Raipur.'

'Scratch.'

Utpal was served a thorough practical definition of 'investigate' as Joseph dragged him around to various friends' places to check out their classmates' photos.

Reactions to Joseph's stated intentions were broadly of two kinds:

Are you nuts? And:

Are you @#$%&*# nuts?

Among the more extreme reactions, Smritimala thought it was sweet but hopeless, and at the other end, Kaushik, who was a little tipsy at the time, literally fell off his chair laughing and broke a glass.

They timed their visit to Asim to coincide with Eid, so they feasted on kababs, biryani and sewai first. Utpal's parents would have probably thrown him out of their house if they found out what he ate at Asim's place, and Asim's parents would have thrown him out of their house if they found out what he ate at Utpal and Joseph's place.

'Who's this?' said Joseph.

'Jonaki Duwara,' said Asim, after a second's thought.

'Nice girl?'

'Wasn't close to her.'

Joseph noted down her name on his notepad and asked, 'Where's she now?'

'Delhi, I think.'

'Got any number or email?'

'Must be on my Orkut friends' list.'

One photo was of Asim and some friends in casuals, in U Turn restaurant, where everything from the restaurant itself to the plates was made of bamboo or other wood. Except the food. Oh, but then, there were the bamboo dishes.

'Who's this?'

'Nandita. She was fun. Slightly crazy too. But from Cotton. So not a grey skirt-wearer.'

'Quite good looking,' said Utpal.

'Her boyfriend was a mega-asshole,' said Asim.

'All the good girls have assholes for boyfriends and all the good boys have bitches for girlfriends,' declared Joseph as he flipped through more photos.

'That reminds me,' said Asim. 'I'm glad you're free of Uma now. I know I met her only two-three times, but she did come across as a bitch. I'd barely gotten introduced to her when she said something bitchy about Parul, who was just ten feet away. And she didn't even know me properly.'

Joseph paused for a second, then simply nodded.

As Joseph went about making enquiries about the girls in the photos, these were some of the replies he got:

Married. Two kids. Gone to Delhi. Settled in Australia. Working in Mumbai. Call centre in Bangalore. With the ILO in Rome. Vanished.

'Vanished? What d'you mean vanished?'

'No one I know knows where she is,' said Arlena.

'Come on. Ten to fifteen years ago it might've been possible for the hero to land up at the heroine's place and find it under lock and key and some neighbour says *'Woh log hamesha hamesha ke liye sheher chhod kar chale gaye.'* But that can't happen nowadays. People can't just vanish in this age of Facebook and Orkut and mobile phones.'

'Unless they change their name.'

'Did she?'

'I don't know. What happened was her parents got divorced, and she and her mom left for Dibrugarh, and from there somewhere else. No idea where.'

'Hmmm...'

And the search went on.

Just had a baby. Preparing for the civils. Some rich boyfriend in Delhi. Teaches at South Point. Married some oldie. Divorced.

'Divorced? Why?'

'Maybe the husband couldn't satisfy her,' said Kaushik as he swept up the broken glass. 'She's in Hyderabad now. By the way, why did Uma dump you?'

'Because I couldn't afford to take her to decent restaurants.'

'In other words, you couldn't satisfy her either.'

'Shuddup.'

'Anyway, whatever happens is for the best. If you don't mind my saying so—hell, I don't care even if you mind—I'll say it—she was a—'

'Bitch,' said Utpal and Joseph together.

Kaushik looked at both of them, then said, 'No. I was going to say she was a nice piece of ass...'

'Oh.'

'... but she really *was* a bitch.'

'Oh.'

Their last stop was their old bandmate Pallav, who played guitar. He was doing his MBA in Kolkata and was currently home on vacation, or he'd have been the first.

'So how many names on your list now?' he asked.

'A hundred and seventy-eight, along with the fourteen from you today.'

'A hundred and seventy-eight! How the hell are you gonna contact all these chicks?'

'Email. Facebook. Orkut.'

'Yeah, no, I get that. I mean—what exactly are you gonna say to them?'

Utpal, who was lying on a bed with his eyes closed, said, "Hi. I'm a psycho loner idiot. My third girlfriend just dumped me. Will you be my fourth and final?"

'I've been thinking of a two-in-one approach,' said Joseph. 'If I just mention straightaway that I think they might be my possible soulmate, it might be a bit too in-your-face. So what I'll do is compose a song and upload it everywhere, and with every mail and message I'll attach a link to the song, so they can hear it and know that I'm actually serious about this and not just a two-bit frustrated aashiq recently escaped from the Tezpur mental hospital. The song will add some artistic depth to the quest.'

So Joseph composed and recorded a song called *In The Year 2002*. The lyrics went thus:

> *In the year 2002 one morning there was a*
> *Girl standing at a bus stop across the street*
> *Maybe Cupid struck 'cause our eyes did meet*
> *And I smiled at her and she smiled back at me*
>
> *I never saw her again after that day*
> *And I don't even remember her face*
> *But I wish we'd meet again*

Hindsight—should've followed up that one glance
Destiny only gives us one chance
Logic and reason say she'll have forgotten
Heart and soul say maybe she was the one
Maybe she's still out there

Joseph got Utpal to sing. Neither of them were very good singers, but Utpal could hold a tune better. Joseph made it in 3 by 4 meter, and kept the guitars acoustic, so that people, no matter what their musical preferences, wouldn't mind giving it a listen.

He took the song to the FM stations in Guwahati. Barring one, the others liked the song and agreed to give it some airplay. One of the programming heads was in fact a fan of their band, having seen them perform once at Nehru Park. The one station that wasn't very positive asked them to get it aired as a sponsored spot. In other words, they wanted money.

'We'll think about it,' said Joseph with a smile, while his thoughts actually were, 'Up yours, mokkel.'

He created a Facebook page called 'The Search For The Girl At The Bus Stop in 2002' and uploaded the song there and on several other websites. He explained who he was, what had happened that morning in 2002, and why he was looking for that girl again.

Then he started messaging and mailing the girls on his list. Within fifteen minutes of starting, he got his first reply.

'Whoa, that's a quick reply,' he said to Utpal, who was seated at the next computer in Moon Internet Café.

"Your song was very cute. But sorry, I'm not that girl. Good luck though." Well, that's encouraging. We're off to a good start.'

'By the way,' said Utpal, 'if and when we do find the girl, are you going to share her with me?'

'What? Of course not!'

'I just thought that because you keep saying "we", maybe "we" could make her our girlfriend and then "we" could get married to her.'

'We can share everything except girlfriends and toothbrushes and underwear.'

Joseph got back to sending more mails. A few minutes later, Utpal said, 'Dude, I just realised something. What if some despo girl hears the song, gets the hots for you and comes and says she was the girl? How'll you know whether she's a fraud or the real deal? And don't say you'll just know or I'll kick you right here right now.'

Joseph's answer was a broad smile.

'What?' said Utpal.

'I'm surprised you sang the song but still haven't understood the full import of the lyrics. Recall the second antara.'

Back home, Joseph played the second antara of the song.

Girl if you happen to hear this song
Rewind the clocks
Flashback to a year now gone

If you remember that moment we had
You'll also remember what happened next
Tell me and I'll know it's you

'Okay,' said Utpal, a bit of understanding dawning. 'Something had happened then?'

'Correct-o.'

'And only that girl would know? This would be her password.'

'Right.'

'What happened? You fell into the drain? A donkey kicked you in the nuts?'

Joseph thought for a second, then said, 'Y'know what, I think it's best if you don't know.'

'What?'

'You might just feel like telling your girlfriend.'

'Asshole, I don't *have* a girlfriend.'

'You might make one in the next few days from all the girls we're approaching.'

'So?'

'She might emotionally blackmail you. "Please, please tell me what the secret is." And she won't let you touch her until you tell her, and then you'll tell her. And then she, being a girl, won't be able to keep it in her stomach, so she'll tell her best friends, then they'll tell their best friends, and soon everyone on the planet will know.'

'Wow,' said a stung Utpal. 'I didn't know you had so much faith in my self-control.'

'Dude, picture this. The two of you are alone in your room. It's raining outside. Some romantic song's playing. Say Jack Black's version of *Let's Get It On*. Your girl removes her jacket to reveal a spaghetti top underneath. Her shoulders are smooth and shiny. You can just see the exposed curve of her waist when she reaches for a bottle of water. Then she leans forward! And then she says, "If you tell me, I'll do anything you want." Tell me, honestly, d'you think you'd be able to resist? Honestly?'

'Yes.'

Joseph tilted his head and raised his eyebrows. Yeah?

'No.'

'There you go.'

'But you know what I honestly think?'

'What?'

'A good alternative career for you would be writing porn.'

'Look, even if this far-fetched situation doesn't happen, you might get drunk some day and blab it out.'

'Okay, fine, enough. So you're really not going to tell me ever?'

'Of course I will. When the time's right. When I get tired of this chase. Or maybe a year later.'

'A year!'

'Whichever happens first.'

As the days went by Joseph received replies from most of the girls he messaged. They were mostly polite.

Hi. No, I'm not the girl.

I'm married.

I like your songs. Let's stay in touch.

Who gave you my email?

You should go for *Indian Idol*.

Get lost, you psycho.

'Whoa. How's that for overreacting?' said Joseph to himself.

One evening at Kaushik's place, Joseph, the usual designated cook, finished preparing pork with bamboo and red chillies and sat down to check his mail. After two no-it-wasn't-me messages followed by crossing the corresponding names off the list, the third message was:

'Hi. I live in Guwahati. Can we meet?'

Joseph read it aloud.

Whoosh. Swish. Utpal and Kaushik jumped over to look.

The profile picture was of a decently pretty girl. The name was Kasturi Bora.

'Cute chick,' said Kaushik.

'Man, she's quite decent-looking,' said Utpal. 'She the one?'

'Can't tell,' said Joseph. 'Let's find out.'

He typed, 'Sure. When and where?'

'We should meet her at the bus stop,' said Utpal.

'Nah. A coffee place is better. And what d'you mean "we"?'

Utpal slapped the back of Joseph's head.

Chapter 4

Into the Drain

'Man, this place is expensive,' said Joseph as he went through the coffee shop's menu. 'I hope she doesn't order anything to eat. I've got just enough for coffee.'

'The bus stop would've been cheaper,' said Utpal.

'Fifty bucks for that tiny brownie! We should've had Daaju's lusi-bhaji at ten bucks.'

'I don't care. I'm hungry. Order any damn thing. We'll split the bill.'

'Thanks. Excuse me, one brownie please.'

As they waited for the brownie, Joseph glanced at the clock. It was 11.25.

'I don't really like late lateefs,' he said.

'Sorry,' said a no-nonsense-without-being-unpleasant female voice behind him. He whirled around startled. It was Kasturi.

'Oh, it's you. H-hi.'

'Hi. Got stuck at Last Gate. Army truck bumped into MLA's car. Very entertaining quarrel.'

'Must've been.'

'Please, sit down,' said Utpal.

'Oh, yeah, yeah. Do sit down.'

'I'm just a little confused,' said Kasturi. 'You're Joseph, right?'

'That's right. This is my friend Utpal, who sang the song.'

'Oh. I thought you'd sung it. Hi.'

'Hi,' said Utpal with a very wide smile.

'So, er, Kasturi, what d'you do?' said Joseph.

'I work in an air-conditioning maintenance office.'

'Hm, sounds very interesting.'

The subsequent light laugh loosened the nervous tension a bit.

'Would you like something to eat?' asked Joseph.

'No thanks. Just had breakfast. Heavy. Ma never lets me leave home without it.'

'How nice,' said Joseph, thinking not just about Kasturi's Ma's heavy breakfast but also about his own light wallet.

The brownie arrived. Utpal put his nose to it, sniffed and made a disapproving face.

'What're you doing?' said Joseph. 'Bad manners.'

'Smells stale,' said Utpal. He took a small bite and made more suspicious faces.

Joseph took a small piece. 'Seems okay to me,' he said, not very confidently.

'I'm telling you, this is stale,' said Utpal, taking another bite.

'Then why the hell are you eating it?'

'Because I'm bloody hungry,' said Utpal as he ate another chunk and grimaced.

'Stop overacting,' said Joseph as he took another bite.

'Why don't you order something more if you're hungry,' said Kasturi. Immediately, both Joseph and Utpal shook their heads simultaneously.

'No, no, no. It's okay,' said Utpal. 'Not so hungry that I'll eat a double dose of stale food.'

'Um, would you like a coffee?' asked Joseph.

'Not really. I had a huge cup of tea at home.'

'Oh,' said Utpal, and turned his gaze to Joseph. 'That's very good. Would *you* like a coffee?'

'Don't really feel like it either,' said Joseph. Thinking quickly, he added, 'Order one for yourself. I'll have a few sips.'

'Right. I need to get the taste of stale brownie out of my mouth,' said Utpal as he suppressed a burp. 'Excuse me! One latte, please.'

'When a girl and guy meet each other for the first time,' said Kasturi, 'it's usually the girl who brings along a friend'.

'Heh-heh, you're right,' said Joseph. 'It's just that Utpal's been with me from day one of this whole—search—and it would be pretty unfair of me not to let him at least say hi.'

'Not to worry,' said Utpal. 'I'll leave you two alone in two minutes.'

'No, no, it's okay. I was just mentioning it as a general observation. Stay. I need to tell you the truth.'

'Oh,' said Joseph. He knew what was coming.

'I'm not the girl from the bus stop.'

The two boys exchanged glances.

'I just sort of, well, I really liked the whole idea behind your search for your soulmate. I wanted to meet whoever was crazy enough to do such a thing. And who also had such a great voice, which turns out to be yours.' The last sentence was directed at Utpal. He practically blushed.

'Well, thank you,' he said. 'I don't sing very well, but thanks.'

'Was it you who composed the song?'

'Er, no. That would be Joseph.'

'Really nice song, Joseph.'

'Thanks.'

An awkward moment followed. No one knew what course such conversations were supposed to take.

'So how many girls have you met so far?' asked Kasturi.

'Well, actually,' said Joseph, 'you're the first girl we've met'.

'"We",' said Utpal, casually tossing out the word.

'Sorry?' said Kasturi.

'Never mind,' said Utpal. 'Joseph has the statistics.'

'Out of 178 possible girls,' said Joseph, 'we've managed to contact 143. Eighty-seven have replied. Forty-one have been nice and encouraging, 43 have been a curt "No!"' Joseph suppressed an odd-tasting burp and frowned before continuing. 'Two have basically said "piss off, psycho", and one has asked to meet, and that would be you.'

'You're crazy,' said Kasturi, 'if you don't mind my saying so'.

'I know.'

'But in a good way. Why don't you just try to meet girls through the normal channels—common friends, parties, weddings?'

'That's exactly what I keep saying to him! Exactly!' said Utpal. BUR-R-P! 'Oh damn. So sorry.'

'It's okay,' said Kasturi.

'Mannerless creature,' said Joseph with mocking contempt. Then he himself let out a short but loud BURP!

'Oh crap. So sorry. The brownie must've been stale.'

'Good morning sir,' said Utpal with vengeance. 'Glad to see you've woken up. Now smell the coffee.'

Right on cue, the coffee was set on the table. But Joseph was starting to look increasingly distressed.

'Are you all right?' asked Kasturi.

'I'm sure he is,' said Utpal, 'having stuffed himself with freshly decayed brownie'.

'I'm all right,' said Joseph, uttering a white lie if ever there was one. 'I just,' he said, stumbling out of his chair, 'need to go to the bathroom'.

Joseph ran and flung open the door of what he thought was the bathroom, but it was the kitchen.

'Where's the bathroom?' he asked the waiter.

'We don't have a bathroom,' was the reply.

'Aargh!'

Joseph ran out of the restaurant. Utpal and Kasturi watched him as he dodged a couple of vehicles and ran across the street to the large drain on the other side and bent over the parapet. Faint sounds of retching and coughing carried over to their ears.

'Well, what can I say?' said Utpal.

'Take the poor fellow some water,' said Kasturi, and handed him a jug.

'Yeah. I'll be right back.'

Utpal went with the jug to Joseph's rescue. As Joseph washed up, Utpal said, 'This is what happens when you don't listen to friends and well-wishers.'

'How come nothing's happened to you?' asked Joseph.

'Maybe I'm more used to crappy food. Feeling better?'

'Yeah. Thanks.'

'Told you it was stale,' said Utpal as he took the jug.

'Even the water tastes funny.'

Utpal lifted the lid of the jug and saw a brown rust-like layer at the bottom. He immediately slammed the lid back down.

'What is it?' said Joseph.

'Never mind.'

'Let me see.'

'You don't wanna.'

Joseph grabbed the jug and looked inside. He turned around towards the drain and threw up a little more.

'When will you start listening to well-wishers?' said Utpal philosophically.

When Joseph had gathered himself enough to merit a place back in civil society, they re-entered the restaurant.

Kasturi had another brownie in hand and was giving the manager a dressing-down. 'You're not the owner, are you?'

The manager, who had a Band-Aid on his chin, shook his head.

'If you were,' said Kasturi, 'you might have taken extra care to ensure that your stuff isn't stale. How are you going to run this place if a customer runs out and throws up every half hour?'

'Sorry Ma'am. This is the first time it's happened.'

The waiter cut in and said to Kasturi, 'Actually, no. Yesterday another chap had fallen ill. He came back in the evening and punched him.'

Which explained the Band-Aid on the chin. The manager winced at the memory. He retorted, 'That fellow had probably eaten something somewhere else!'

'Rubbish!' said the waiter, raising his volume proportionately. 'It's all this stale stuff that you don't let us throw away! I used to run my tea stall in the village better than you run this place!'

'Then get out! Get lost! Go back to your damned tea stall!'

'Fine! I can make better tea for three bucks than your shitty thirty-rupee tea! Pay me for this month's work!'

'Piss off! This isn't your baap ka hotel!'

'Oi! D'you know what I do to people who bring my baap into things!'

'No! What d'you do!'

Wham! The waiter's fist landed on the manager, who promptly disappeared behind the counter. If there was any consolation the manager could have derived from being punched in the face the second time in two days, it was that the second Band-Aid would now be on the other side of his chin, making the facial decor symmetrical, since this waiter was left-handed, or in this particular instance, left-fisted.

As the left-fisted waiter stormed out, Utpal looked at Joseph and said, 'Let's go.'

Once outside, Kasturi said to Utpal, 'You'd better take him home.'

'I'll be all right. Feeling okay now,' said Joseph.

'Quite a weird meet we've had eh?' said Kasturi. 'Can we stay in touch?'

'Sure,' said Utpal. 'Give me your number.'

After the exchange of numbers, Joseph asked, 'By any chance, do you sing?'

'Not really. Only bathroom and bedroom.'

Joseph nodded.

As Kasturi walked away, Joseph took out his list and said, 'Another one bites the dust.'

'Hmmm...' said Utpal, not really listening. He was gazing after Kasturi.

Chapter 5
A Year Goes By

A YEAR WENT BY.

Chapter 6

The Minor Benefits of Not Getting Seduced Too Easily

In the year that went by, to briefly summarise, Joseph did get himself a brand new bike, albeit second-hand, or pre-owned, as dealers like to euphemistically say. To keep the wolves and the landlord from the door, he also started teaching guitar and English and Maths and whatever else class X students wanted to learn. He remembered almost everything till his matriculation, but practically zilch after that. He recorded guitar tracks for a few songs, only one of which he himself liked, and played at a few Bihu functions, where most of the audience was usually too drunk or too impolite to bother clapping in appreciation.

The one major change in Utpal's life was that he had started dating Kasturi. Several young men unconsciously drift towards women who can whip them into shape and keep them on the straight and narrow. Utpal and Kasturi were one each of these respective species.

Around a month before the completion of a year since the search had started, Kasturi introduced Joseph to Runima, a friend of hers from college days. She was slim and quite attractive by any standards; the kind of girl who would be used to having boys easily fall for her.

Runima was instantly attracted to Joseph's bloke-with-guitar-and-aching-heart persona, but she tried to play it cool and hard to get, which unfortunately didn't work in her favour as Joseph didn't even try the 'get' part of hard to get, let alone the try hard part. He was polite, and they went together for a couple of movies, but he somehow never felt at ease with her, nor could he put his finger on the exact reason why.

One Sunday morning in Moon Internet Café, Utpal was checking his email and simultaneously talking to his beloved.

'She said she's going to seduce him,' said Kasturi, referring to Runima's agenda for the day.

'Really?' said Utpal. 'That's bold. I like it. Good for Joseph. The poor fellow hasn't had any action in nearly—hm—eighteen months? How's she planning to do it—I mean, not what positions—the seduction part?'

'She said she'd be wearing her very low-cut red top.'

'Uh-huh. And?'

'Wear a short skirt and sit a little carelessly.'
'Uh-huh. And?'

Something in Utpal's tone struck Kasturi as inappropriate. She quickly cut into his visualisations. 'Hello, you're not picturing her, are you?'

'Eh, no,' said Utpal, jerked out of his almost-beginning reverie.

'You'd better not, for your own sake.'

'No, no, my dear, I'm loyal to you. Physically spiritually mentally.'

'Good.'

A sudden impulse to look up the Facebook page on Joseph's bus stop girl arose in Utpal. It had been nearly two months since he had last checked. He opened the page.

There was a new message.

They say men can't do more than one thing at a time. Utpal tried to defy the wisdom of the ages, quietly reading the message and simultaneously talking to Kasturi. He said, 'Ever since I met you, my days and nights have turned into—shit!'

If life were a cartoon, Utpal's eyeballs would have popped out of their sockets and bounced and dangled about like they were on springs.

'What!' said Kasturi with understandable indignation.

'Shit!'

'What!'

'No, not you. I mean, there's a new message here for Joseph. When did Runima say she was gonna see him?'

'That was half an hour ago.'

'Oh shit!'

'What happened?'

'Let me call you in a minute.'

Utpal cut the line and called Joseph. Teet-teet tring-tring toot-toot... no answer.

'Dammit,' said Utpal and scrambled towards the door.

As he ran out, Moon the café owner yelled at him, 'Money! Money!'

'Later! Later!' yelled back Utpal, and started running and redialling Joseph's number. There was still no answer.

'Oh please don't be doing it with the phone on silent please,' said Utpal into his cell as he huffed and puffed and blew the house down—I mean, huffed and puffed and ran. Talking to the ring tone, as though his voice might somehow break some technological barriers, he said, 'Joseph, if you're starting to do it or are doing it, stop!... And if you've already done it... don't do it again!'

Five calls went unanswered during Utpal's increasingly panicked ten-minute run to their flat. He pounced on the doorbell and rang it repeatedly, muttering, 'Please please don't already have done it.'

He heard Joseph's voice say, 'Coming, coming!', and the irritation in his voice could mean only one thing—that he had been interrupted in the middle of some intense activity.

Joseph opened the door and Utpal's heart sank. He was wearing only a towel and his whole body was wet with sweat. Over his shoulder, beyond the hall and the corridor, on the bed in Joseph's room, was seated the seductress Runima.

'Oh shit. You've already done it,' said Utpal, face fallen.

'Done what?'

'Kama Sutra.'

'No, idiot. I was bathing.'

'With her?'

'No, mokkel. Alone. What's the problem?'

'You really haven't done anything? Smooching-wooching-groping-loving-touching-squeezing?'

'Shuddup, asshole, no! What's the matter?'

'Kasturi told me her plan was to seduce you today.'

Joseph cast a glance at Runima, who was busy texting, then said to Utpal, 'So? I got that feeling too. Not such a bad idea. What's the problem then? You found out she has AIDS?'

'No.'

'Then d'you want her as well?'

Utpal grabbed Joseph's arm and led him inside. 'Hurry up and put on your underwear and whatever other optional clothes you want. We're going to the Panbazar Baptist church.'

Joseph processed the instructions for a second, then said, 'Which mad dog bit you?'

'Okay, now tell me. After the girl at the bus stop smiled at you, something happened to your pants. Is that right?'

Joseph was suitably astounded. 'Who told you?'

'Yes or no?'

'Yes. Who told you?'

'Yes! Yes!' said Utpal, punching the air in triumph. 'Dude, we have half an hour if you wanna meet her.'

'Dammit! Who?'

'Your long-lost dream girl.'

Joseph grabbed Utpal's collar and said, 'You're not making a mokkel of me, are you?'

'Mokkel, I'm serious. She said she'd be at the church till about eleven. You'd better hurry.'

Joseph took a hard look at Utpal's face, decided he indeed wasn't making a mokkel of him, then darted into his room.

Joseph's putting on his pants was the exact opposite of what Runima had planned. With a none-too-pleased tone, she asked, 'What is it?'

'Runima, I'm sorry,' said Joseph as he sprayed deodorant on himself, 'but I have to rush. Utpal says we may have found an old friend.'

'You mean your bus stop girl?'

'Yes,' said Joseph, hopping around with one leg attempting to enter its trouser. 'Pass me my shirt please.'

Runima picked up the freshly ironed shirt on the bed beside her, angrily crumpled it, then hurled it at Joseph's face. The sudden loss of visual orientation caused Joseph to lose his balance and he fell to the floor with a mild crash.

'Sorry 'bout that,' said Joseph, removing the shirt from his face, but she was already gone.

A gaping Utpal had seen the action from the hall. As Runima walked past him in a huff, he said, 'See you later.'

'Shut up!' she said. 'And piss off!'

She slammed the door on her way out.

'Wow,' said Utpal. 'She must've been in some heat.' Then cupping his hands in the direction of the door, he said at low volume, without really intending for her to hear, 'Hey, if he doesn't want your services, I'm available and ready 24/7.'

The door swung open. Runima was still there, having just put on her shoes. She took a couple of rapid strides towards Utpal, who said apologetically, 'Oh you're still here? I was just—'

Thwack-o! Or something similar, was the sound of the slap. Then the slapper stormed out.

'—joking,' finished Utpal. Then he went into Joseph's room, still clutching his cheek, and said, 'Dude, she slapped me.'

'She crumpled my shirt and threw it at my face.'

'Screw your shirt. She slapped me. On the face.'

'Would you have preferred it on the arse? What did you say to her?'

'I was just being sympathetic and helpful.'

'More likely lecherous and lustful.'

'That's the first time a girl's slapped me so hard. And she probably meant it for you, not me. I just happened to be in the wrong place at the wrong time.'

'Will you shut up about her,' said Joseph as they walked out and locked the door. 'She can go to blazes. Tell me what's happened. Somebody messaged?'

'I just thought I'd check the Facebook page. Been a long time. And there was this message. It came in on—Thursday.'

'What's her name?' said Joseph, trying to kickstart his bike. It firmly refused.

'Aastha. Aastha Mishra.'

'Mishra?'

'Yup.'

'What's she look like?'

'Dunno. The profile picture was of Asterix's chief's wife—what was her name?'

'Impedimenta. A comicbook reader—hm—I like that.'

Joseph kicked and kicked but his bike stubbornly refused to start.

'Dammit! Push, please.'

'You push!' said Utpal. 'I've already done a lot of running. And got slapped too.'

'How the hell are they related?'

'Both were because of you.'

Joseph let out an exasperated sound effect. Utpal mounted the bike and Joseph started pushing. After a couple of runs, it finally started.

As they drove through Chandmari, Utpal said, 'Short message. "Hi Joseph. It was your pants, right? If you would like to meet up, come on Sunday to the Panbazar Baptist Church between 9 and 11am."'

'That's all? No details?'

'Nope.'

'Did you check out her profile?'

'Just the info page. Member of St Mary's School 2000, I Love *Calvin & Hobbes*, Celine Dion, Jack Black, *Tintin*, Arjun Pathania and some other pages.'

'Tintin? Jack Black? I'm starting to like her already. Except for the Arjun Pathania bit.'

'Yeah. Except for that.'

As they turned the corner at Handique Girls' College, much to Joseph's horror, the bike started coughing and sputtering. He looked at the fuel gauge. It was sub-empty.

'What da health!' he said. 'Didn't you fill any petrol?'

'I did,' said Utpal, 'but I think I forgot to put the valve back on "on".'

'Mokkel!'

The bike sputtered to a halt right in front of the hostel. Three girls having sugarcane juice became spectators to the sight of an embarrassed Joseph trying to start the bike with its very last droplets of fuel. He noticed Utpal trying to catch their eye.

'Shameless mokkel,' said Joseph, 'you've got a girlfriend now'.

'I'm only looking. Not gonna ask for their numbers.'

'Dammit! Help me push now. It's purely your fault this time.'

Luckily, just around the corner the road sloped downhill till Cotton College's RKB Hostel, so they sat and let gravity propel them some distance. Their combined momentum ran out just in front of BKB auditorium, after which they had to push for a half kilometre or so.

Joseph was sure that the increased frequency and amplitude of his heartbeat couldn't have been only because of pushing the bike—that was something he was used to. This was a special occasion. Would this girl turn out to be the girl he had seen nine years ago? And even if not, would she and he, like Kasturi and Utpal, still have enough chemistry between them to consider a future together?

He looked at his watch as they hauled the bike into the parking area of the century-old church. It was already 11.

'If she's gone,' said Joseph, 'I'll—'
'Sh! Someone's singing.'

Joseph listened. There they were—the faint strains of a female voice, accompanied by a single acoustic guitar, coming from inside the church.

The two of them walked without a word. The day was cold, but bright and sunny. The gravel walkway was lined with palm trees on both sides. A small graveyard was at the far end, a few freshly laid flowers adding colour to the white and grey crosses and tombstones.

Joseph was hoping with all his might that this voice, whose richness and range were becoming more and more apparent as they closed in, belonged to the very girl they had come to meet. If he had been the praying sort he would have prayed for it.

A jarring note, only in Joseph's brain and not literally, was hit by a male voice that was singing harmonies as flawlessly as the female voice. This immediately prickled Joseph. There were two kinds of males he was jealous of—those who could draw and those who could sing, the latter more acutely. There used to be a third category—those who could play guitar, but Joseph had surmounted this by very wisely following the old adage of joining 'em if you can't beat 'em.

When Joseph stepped into the church, he saw that almost all the people were Nagas—about sixty of them. It was a sparsely furnished and decorated church, not that Joseph had any time to take the décor in. Within half a second, his eyes had fixated on the girl onstage whose voice was responsible for everyone feeling, at least for those few minutes, that the world was a wonderful place and it was great to be alive.

He cast a quick glance at the man who was playing guitar and singing beside her. Some old but good-looking father-figure type. Looked Naga too. Not the competition, Joseph thought, and relaxed. He whispered to Utpal:

'I told you she'd be a great singer.'

'How d'you know that's her?'

'Does anyone else in this room look like a Mishra?'

Utpal looked around. All Naga faces with one or two exceptions.

'No.'

They sat down beside an elegantly dressed woman.

'Excuse me, Aunty,' whispered Joseph, 'who's that girl?'

'I think her name is Aastha.'

Joseph mumbled thanks and smiled. He looked at Utpal and smiled some more. Then he noticed the father-figure guitarist was also smiling, but at Aastha, and too much at that. Lecherous old man, thought Joseph.

He refocused his attention on Aastha. Was it really her? After nine years? If everything else about her was as wonderful as her singing, this was probably a dream too good to be true. She hit all her notes with perfect accuracy, both in pitch and tempo. The song, *Nothing but the Blood of Jesus*, was a gospel song and therefore didn't have any operatic high notes in it, but from the way Aastha so cleanly projected her voice, Joseph was sure she could easily hit high notes without much effort. And her rich yet subtle vibrato added wonderful texture.

Joseph smiled and sighed. Aastha was slim and about 5'4', although he could be sure only when she stood up. She was the colour of freshly-ground coffee that had a glow about it. When she smiled, her teeth were almost all perfect except for a crooked and pointed lower canine that suggested fanged mischief. Her eyes, Joseph thought, were the kind that one could simply look into and grow auto-hypnotised by. Joseph couldn't stop smiling. Now if only she's single—

The song ended. People clapped heartily. Aastha and the guitar-wielding man smiled and bowed to the crowd.

Then the oldie hugged Aastha and kissed her on the cheek!

Joseph bristled. He wasn't her boyfriend or anything—he hadn't even met her yet—but he couldn't help feeling a slight green-coloured burn somewhere in his chest. What was worse, Aastha didn't seem to mind the kiss at all.

The two of them got off the stage and a preacher took their place.

'Excuse me, Aunty,' whispered Joseph, 'but who was the man playing guitar?'

'I think that's her husband.'

'What!' said Joseph loudly. It was actually a whisper, but by the standards of a quiet church gathering, a loud whisper is plain simple loud. People within a radius of five people all turned to stare at him. Even the Aunty was scowling. Utpal was hiding his face and making sure he wasn't associated with this mannerless loony in any way.

'Sorry,' whispered Joseph to the public. They turned away and directed their attention back to the preacher.

'Assssssss—' hissed Utpal as quietly and sharply as possible.

'Sorry,' said a very shocked Joseph.

'—hole!'

Joseph stared at Aastha and the oldie, who were now seated in the front row. Her husband! Her husband!!! That doddering old fool was her husband! Joseph's fairy tale future was shattered by that one word. All his dreams—crushed.

He couldn't bear it any more. 'Let's go,' he said to Utpal, and out they went.

On the steps, Joseph sat with his face in his hands, every bit the picture of the nipped-in-the-bud lover. Utpal put a sympathetic hand on his shoulder and said, 'Sorry, mate.'

Joseph didn't reply. Utpal brought him one of the plastic glasses of water laid out on the table outside. He reckoned it would be a good idea not to let dehydration pile upon heartbreak.

Joseph quietly drank the water, then fiddled with the glass.

'That buddha?' said Utpal. 'Her husband? Thundering typhoons!'

'Tharki old tycoons,' said Joseph. 'I knew there had to be a catch.'

'Seriously, what's wrong with girls? Why do they end up with old men who've got one foot in a freshly dug grave? They like to call them "mature". Mature my royal ass. Old is the word.'

'Maybe it's the money.'

'Yeah. Guys our age aren't always financially secure. So girls our age dump us and flock to rich old men.'

The service had ended and people were coming out of the church.

'Story of my life,' said Joseph. 'Part four. The sequel. No, the quadruquel. Even the never-was girlfriend turned out to be a gold digger who'd already gone and married a rich old man.'

'Look at the flip side. When we're ten years older or so, some girl will dump *her* poor sod of a boyfriend and come to marry *us* instead.'

Joseph didn't answer. Utpal continued his cheer-up speech. 'Look, all's not lost. Maybe that buddha husband will have a heart attack soon and she'll be free to be with you. And as a bonus, she'll have all his money.'

'Did you get a good look at him? He looks fitter and healthier than you and me combined. He'll probably die fifty years after us... Damn all rich buddhas!' And with that, Joseph flung the glass onto the ground.

'Are temper tantrums a frequent indulgence for you?' said a female voice behind them.

It was Aastha. She looked amused.

Joseph was flustered. He blurted, 'Er, no—not really. Just reserved for festivals and special occasions.'

Aastha chuckled. Joseph was gratified that she had found his quip funny and pained that she already had someone else to make her laugh on a more regular basis.

'So what's the occasion this time?' said Aastha.

'Well—just that one year of efforts have come to goo.'

'What d'you mean?'

'Excuse me for saying this—we're only meeting for the first time—but what the hell's the big deal with rich "mature" men? I mean, what is it about them that so many girls seem to just flock to them? Is it really just the money? I mean, can you really spend life with someone twenty years older than you?'

Aastha considered the rant for a second, then said, 'Why're you asking me this?'

'Well, because I've remembered you for nine years of my life and spent a year looking for you—if it is you, that is—and now that you turn up, I find you're hitched to some rich old geezer like every other girl.'

'Rich old geezer? Who're you talking about?'

Joseph spotted the 'old geezer' opening a car door.

'That senior citizen's pension plan over there,' said Joseph.

Aastha looked and said, 'Him?'

'Yeah.'

Aastha waved at the senior citizen. He waved back, and then she said to him:

'Papa, you carry on home. This is the guy. I'll come later.'

'Okay, beta,' was the reply.

Papa then got into the car and started it. When he was out of the church grounds, Aastha turned back to Joseph.

'P-p-p-ppp-papa?' he stuttered.

'Yes, and that's not my nickname for him. He actually happens to be my father.'

'B-b-b-bbb-but that woman said he was your husband.'

'Who?'

'The woman we were sitting next to.'

'Must've been a misunderstanding.'

Joseph would have wished that the earth would split open and swallow him up, but being a sci-fi fan, he wished for aliens to kidnap him immediately and erase the last fifteen minutes of his memory so he could start over. He felt his ears grow hot and his feet grow cold with embarrassment.

'So that's why you were steaming?' said Aastha.

'Uh, y-y-yes. Sorry about that. Stupid misinformation campaign.'

'That's okay.' Thankfully, Aastha hadn't taken offence.

'But how come you don't look anything like him? I mean, he looks like a proper Naga.'

'Papa's mother was Sikkimese and his dad and my mother were from Jharkhand. We're as cocktail as can be.'

'So, um, he's actually your father. Well, that's a huge relief. Er—would you like some water?'

'Yeah,' said Aastha, and picked up a glass before Joseph had the chance to be chivalrous.

'How did you get to know of this—our search?' said Joseph.

'A friend told me. She'd downloaded the song. I got back just two weeks ago or I'd have heard it sooner. I've been in Hyderabad the last few years.'

Before Joseph could ask what she did and had been doing, Utpal cut in and said, 'Do you have a boyfriend?'

'Had. Long time ago. You're Utpal, right?'

'Yeah,' said Utpal, slightly embarrassed. Celebrity, no matter how minor, wasn't something he could handle with adroitness.

'You have a nice voice.'

'Thanks.'

'But not as nice as yours,' said Joseph quickly, not wanting Aastha to go the Kasturi way. Boy, would that be complicated!

'Well, thank you. Why d'you seem so flustered?'

'Wouldn't I be?' said Joseph. 'I just made a majorly embarrassing slip-up—thinking your father was your husband. Yikes.'

'That's quite all right. Although I can't say it happens all the time.'

They shared a chuckle, then Utpal said, 'Are you the girl from the bus stop in 2002?'

Aastha took a second, then said, 'What if I am?'

'Well,' said Utpal, 'this hero's been looking for you for nearly a year now, and I've suffered along with him'.

'At least you found a girlfriend,' said Joseph.

'Now you've found yours too,' said Utpal.

Simultaneously, Joseph said 'Shut up' and Aastha said 'Hang on'.

'We've only just met,' said Joseph.

'Listen,' said Aastha. 'I don't want you to have any expectations from me. None. The honest truth is I just wanted to meet the guy who would go to so much trouble to find a girl.'

'But are you really that girl?' asked Utpal. 'What's the password?'

'Eh?'

'I mean, what happened to his pants that day?'

Chapter 7

Look Left, Look Right, Look Left Again, then Cross—If there are no Vehicles

Eighteen-year-old Joseph stood at the corner on the Zoo-Narengi Road side of the Tiniali, waiting for a chance to cross. His eyes drifted for a second to the people on the other side, some of whom had just gotten off a bus.

Magic happens just once in a lifetime, or maybe twice for some lucky people, and several times for philanderers, at least in their imagination. For Joseph, that morning was his magic moment, although he would fully realise it only years and years later.

Some invisible string guided his gaze to a particular face at the bus stop on the other side. It was a girl—neither angel nor supermodel—but the instant that Joseph looked at her, she looked right back at him, and it felt like they had locked eyes not across a busy street but across an arm's length. Thud-thud went Joseph's heart. His normal reaction would have been to avert his gaze, lest the girl in question think he was leering, but this time was different—it was like her eyes had yanked him in and weren't letting go. A very slight smile formed on the girl's face and she looked away for an instant, but the shy smile was still there. Then, as if she couldn't resist, she looked right back at Joseph again, still smiling, and this time, Joseph couldn't help but smile back. He knew that he was grinning like an idiot but he simply couldn't turn it off.

This ethereal encounter lasted less than ten seconds but would live on in Joseph's memories for the next nine years.

Then the traffic eased up on the girl's side of the road and people around her started walking across, so she started too.

The thud-thud in Joseph's heart doubled in frequency. She was coming this side and he was supposed to be going that side. What should he do? Say hi? Ask her name? Or do something stupid like follow her? But then he already had a girlfriend, and he wasn't a believer in spare-tyre relationships.

She again looked at him when she reached the road divider. Lost in her eyes, Joseph forgot the rules of the road and took a couple of steps without looking left and right and left again. He was looking straight ahead.

A young milkman, or milkboy to be more accurate, was whizzing by on his bicycle at a pace highly unadvisable for a cycle with a large jar of milk hung on its right side. On the left side was a metal hook for hanging another jar. As the cycle passed by an unseeing Joseph, this hook somehow got entangled in his trouser pocket and rrriiiiipppppp… !

It took a few seconds for Joseph to come back to earth. He looked at his pants. The right leg had been completely ripped apart from the pocket down, making him look like Helen in a cabaret dance.

'Oi!' he shouted at the milkboy, who was already turning the corner.

'What oi!' he shouted back. 'Don't stare at girls when crossing the road!'

A couple of onlookers tittered. Joseph didn't have a good comeback because the little twerp was right, after all.

He again looked at the girl. She was smiling at him. And that one smile told Joseph that she knew this had happened because he had been staring at her. He smiled back. Something might have happened at that instant— she might have asked whether he was okay, Joseph might have said something witty and self-deprecating. They might have gotten introduced. Dated. Married. Raised children who might have altered the course of world history by discovering a cure for cancer or becoming post-independent India's first genocidal despot. But none of these were to be. At least not then.

An elderly gentleman beside Joseph laid a hand on his shoulder and said, 'Son, are you okay?'

The spell was broken.

'Yes Uncle, I'm fine,' said Joseph. He looked at his pants again. Even his underwear was showing. And because it was light brown, people looking from a distance would think it was skin. They would later point to him and tell each other, 'That kid doesn't wear underwear.'

Preservation of self and reputation took precedence. What was he to do now in this highly embarrassing state? He'd obviously have to go back home, but he couldn't go back like this either. He looked around and saw a stationery-photocopy shop behind him. Idea.

'Dada, can I borrow your stapler?' said Joseph to the man in the shop.

'Are you hurt?' said the man as he handed Joseph a stapler.

'I don't think. Just the pants.'

Joseph stapled his trouser leg from top to bottom. A weird solution, but he could at least get home without being a total laughing-stock.

He thanked the shopkeeper, then stepped out and looked around.

She was gone.

Chapter 8

Soulmates and Sole Mates

This was the pattern of Utpal's laughter when he had heard the story of the ripped pants: Ha... Ha ha... Ha ha ha ha. Buwahahahahahaha...

'It's not that funny,' said Joseph.

'Are you nuts? It's hysterical! I'm imagining you dancing in the middle of Zoo-Narengi Road, showing leg, like Helen ha ha ha ha...'

'All right, all right, you deserve a laugh.'

'This sort of weird thing always seems to happen to you... ha ha ha...'

After Utpal's laughter had subsided to moderate levels, Aastha said to Joseph, 'Well, what now? Now that we've actually met. I mean, what were your intentions if you actually found the girl?'

'Dangerous intentions,' said Utpal.

'Shut up,' said Joseph. He tried to gather and organise his multitude of thoughts. 'I wanted to find the girl because I believed she might have been my soulmate—the one girl with whom my story would end at "and they lived happily ever after".'

'Just because of that one smile?' said Aastha.

'It must have meant something. Why would you smile at a random stranger?'

'I can't remember.'

'Something must've clicked between us.'

'I don't believe in love at first sight anymore. That's how it was with my ex-boyfriend.'

'Okay. So what's the story there?'

'Well, I saw him. Was floored right away. For the first few months it was okay. Then gradually I realised we really had nothing in common. I simply hung on for two years, trying to make it work.'

'What d'you mean, nothing in common?'

'Well, on our first month anniversary, his card said, "To my Saline Dion".'

Both Utpal and Joseph burst out laughing.

'Then I realised he actually used to get jealous when people applauded my singing at college functions, et cetera.'

'What a nutcase,' said Joseph.

'I told him I definitely would never stop singing, so we reached a compromise. He stopped coming to my shows, and I never told him about them.'

'What an assh—I mean, total fool,' said Utpal.

'It's all right. He was an asshole,' said Aastha.

'When did you break up?' asked Joseph.

'Three years ago.'
'Hm. What was the last straw?'
'Our wedding.'
'What! You got married?'
'No. We broke up on our wedding day.'
'Nick of time, eh? What happened?'

Chapter 9

The Exciting Wedding Video

Kavita Marriage Hall happened to be diagonally opposite the corner where Joseph and Aastha had had their first encounter. On a chilly November evening in 2007, the engagement board read in shiny golden letters, 'AASTHA WEDS MONTY'.

Dressed in bridal finery, Aastha was seated with a few of her friends in a room on the first floor, waiting for the pandit-appointed hour to get married.

In walked her father, a laptop in hand. The incongruity of the laptop, which happened to be her fiance Monty's, wasn't lost upon Aastha.

'Ladies,' said Mr Mishra to Aastha's friends, 'would you please give us a minute'.

'What's the matter?' said Aastha.

Mr Mishra gave her an I'll-tell-you nod. When her friends had gone, he sat down beside her, smiled a weird smile, and said, 'Your father-in-law-to-be-outlaw is asking for five lakh in cash.'

In keeping with the dramatic requirements of the moment, Aastha flung off her ghoonghat and said, 'What!'

If this were a scene in the saas-bahu serial being watched by Moon the internet café owner in the first chapter, Aastha would have said 'What!' from at least five different angles. Tilt up—what! Swoosh pan left—what! Swoosh pan right—what! Tilt down—what! Rotate upside down—what!

Mr Mishra's smile wasn't because he couldn't believe this was actually happening to him, but because he had always felt Monty was a dumb lunkhead who had forgotten to stick around when IQ was being handed out, and his father was a classless, tasteless, crass fatass who probably haggled even with beggars. He had voiced his concerns, but having raised Aastha all by himself, it was his wont to defer to her wishes, so if it was this particular brand of lunkhead that she wanted to marry, then it was this particular brand of lunkhead that she would marry. The reason for his gallows humour at the moment was that finally, here was the first chance for Aastha to observe a demonstration of her future family's true colours.

'What!' said Aastha again, even more vehemently this time.

Mr Mishra didn't elaborate immediately. Instead, he savoured the moment, thoroughly sympathetic, but also relishing his daughter's long-overdue outrage-cum-epiphany.

'You aren't joking, are you?' said Aastha.

Mr Mishra shook his head and said, 'He gave me Monty's laptop to make the transfer. Should I do it?'

'What! Of course not!'

Mr Mishra finally let himself laugh. 'Thank God! You *are* my daughter after all. Good. Now I can call him all the names I've been wanting to call him since the day they came to our place. Crooked senile cheap swindling extortionist fat bastard.'

Aastha stood up, her head a little fuzzy. She chipped in with some abuses of her own. 'Bloody sonofabitch asshole two-faced two-timing motherf—'

'Ho!' said Mr Mishra. 'Control.'

'Sorry, Papa,' she said, snapping into action. 'Where are they?' she said, taking the laptop.

'Downstairs.'

'I can't believe this! Do they think this is an '80s film!'

Laptop in hand, Aastha barged into the mandap area, walking the walk of a woman likely to erupt at any moment.

Her prospective husband and father-out-law were talking merrily to some of their relatives. Aastha grabbed Monty's arm and pulled him aside.

'What's this about your dad demanding money from my dad?' she whispered sharply.

'Yeah,' said Monty slowly.

'Yeah? What d'you mean, yeah? What kind of answer is that, yeah? Did I ask you whether you're wearing pyjamas? Is your dad asking my dad for dowry?'

Monty shrugged and said, 'Who said dowry? I guess Dad just wants some kind of back-up fund for us.'

Aastha almost laughed. 'That's the worst euphemism I've heard in my life. Back-up fund, indeed. And you're okay with this?'

'Yeah… I guess.'

Before Aastha could let loose another fusillade, Monty's father sneaked up, a wide sleazy smile on his face.

'So, beti, has the transfer been made?' he said.

Aastha gave him a contemptuous glance, then totally ignoring him, asked Monty, 'So you're not going to marry me if my dad doesn't pay your dad?'

At this stage, people had started sensing that something out of the ordinary was happening. Most weddings are dull and drab affairs, where everyone puts on plastic smiles, gifts what ends up as either the sixth cheap pressure cooker or the seventeenth crockery set, eats, comments on the quality of the food and then pushes off before their cheek muscles start aching from all the forced geniality. A quarrel at a wedding makes for wonderful enlivening of proceedings. And if it happens to be between bride and groom, ah! Sone pe suhaaga!

The wedding cameraman, a young chap bored stiff of doing weddings of overdressed couples and their fat relatives, immediately sensed that he finally had a chance to shoot some real solid drama, and he promptly but discreetly pointed his camera at the primary players.

'It's for your own benefit, beti,' Monty's dad was saying.

'Give me a straight answer—yes or no?' said Aastha to Monty.

Monty weakly looked at his father, who folded his arms, literally stuck his nose up, and said, 'No.'

Aastha cast Monty a questioning glance. He just shrugged.

'Wow,' said Aastha, laughing lightly. 'I must be a really shitty judge of character not to have guessed that you'd turn out to be such a wimp… Okay, you want the transfer to made with this laptop?'

'Yes,' said Monty's father.

Aastha took the laptop, lifted it high over her head, and hurled it **on**to the floor.

SMASH!

'What're you doing!' said Monty.

Everyone's heads had turned their way by now. The most excited of all was the cameraman, who was grinning ear to ear at the priceless footage being recorded for posterity.

Aastha looked around and spotted a carpenter who had been hammering **in** some nails somewhere. She grabbed the hammer, turned back to Monty and said, 'Ever hear of the expression, "Bang for your buck"? Well, here goes, you little f@#$!'

Aastha dropped down to her knees and brought the hammer down on the laptop with all her might. Bang! Bang! Crunch! Smash!

'Oi!' shouted Monty. 'What're you doing! Stop!'

'She's mad!' said his dad. 'After marriage that would've been your head instead! And even a helmet wouldn't have saved you. Let's go!'

Monty's father almost bumped into Mr Mishra as he turned around. He said, 'Mishra, this is what you've taught your daughter to be? A mad version of Ma Kali?'

'Well, you greedy little scumbag,' said Mr Mishra, 'unlike you, I haven't taught my child to be a eunuch'.

Aastha gave the laptop one final stomp.

'You'll regret this,' said Monty's father, and started for the exit. Mr Mishra couldn't resist a childish impulse and he stuck his foot out. Monty's father tripped and crashed into a row of plastic chairs.

'Dad!' said Monty, who had seen the tripping. He turned to Mr Mishra and said, 'You—!'

Aastha brandished the hammer right in front of his nose and said, 'What, eh? What?'

Monty backed off and picked up his heavy father.

'You're mad!' he said as they made for the door.

'F%$# off, asshole!'

'Beta, language,' said Mr Mishra.

'Sorry, Papa. Just for today,' said Aastha, then again opened the abuse tap. 'Get lost, fartface! I can't believe I wasted two years of my life with a ball-less ass-less chhakka like you!'

Just before he was out the door, Monty tried for a Parthian shot. 'Crazy bitch!'

Aastha picked up the largest chunk of the deceased laptop and hurled it in Monty's direction. He had already darted out, though, and the chunk crashed into the signboard, which very wisely didn't put up a fight and immediately fell down.

A sudden silence had settled inside the marriage hall. All the commotion and sounds of vehicles starting were outside.

Aastha looked around, then hugged her father. 'Sorry, Papa.' A couple of tears started falling.

'Sorry for what? I'm proud of you... Look at me... *I'd* have been sorry if you'd married that idiot.'

And for a few moments, daughter took refuge in the arms of father.

The super-delighted cameraman had been following the action all along, having even gone outside to record the reactions of the groom's side and their vehicles leaving in total disarray. He came back in and saw the wonderful emotional ending being provided by the bride and her father and nearly broke into tears himself, not out of empathy, but because he couldn't believe his luck.

Then he pointed his camera at the fallen notice board.

The piece had hit the 'E' in 'WEDS' and turned it clockwise, so it now looked like 'AASTHA WMDs MONTY'.

Satisfied, the cameraman took a pause and turned to the nearest human being, who happened to be the carpenter, and said, 'I'm going to sell this to some reality show.'

Chapter 10

Soulmates & Sole Mates—II

'Congratulations,' said Joseph with new respect in his voice. He extended a hand. 'I'm proud to have met you.'

'Same here,' said Utpal, and offered his hand as well.

'If a movie's ever made on you, it could be called *The Psycho Bride Who Chased Away Her Groom With A Hammer*.'

'Well, I'm rather hungry,' said Aastha. 'How about you guys?'

'We were born hungry,' said Joseph.

'What d'you wanna eat?'

'Momos?' said Utpal.

'You guys eat at Pirish?'

Utpal and Joseph looked at each other and smiled. That was their favourite place for momos in the whole wide world. They had started eating there when momos were eighteen bucks a plate, had tried momos in many other towns and cities including some of the metros where six tiny momos came for some obscene price like seventy or ninety, but found none they liked more than the momos at Pirish or its next-door sister restaurant Momo Ghar.

'D'you eat there often?' said Joseph.

'Yup. Averaging once a week since 1999.'

'How come we've never bumped into each other?' said Joseph.

'Probably just didn't notice each other.'

'Let's discuss serendipity later,' said Utpal. 'I'm hungry. Let's move.'

The bike still had to be pushed to the nearest petrol pump, which was unfortunately a kilometre and a half away in Ambari, less than a javelin throw from Pirish restaurant.

Utpal generously offered to push first so that Joseph could talk with Aastha without strain.

'Before anything else,' said Utpal as they walked out of the church grounds, 'please tell me one thing. Which college were you in? Swadeshi?'

'No,' said Aastha.

'Maria's?'

'No.'

'Faculty?' offered Joseph.

'No. Handique.'

'What!' said both Joseph and Utpal.

'But—but Handique doesn't even have uniforms, leave alone grey skirts,' said Utpal. 'Everyone wears salwar-kameez.'

Aastha smiled and said, 'That day was a Sunday.'

'What!' said the two boys again.

'Yup. I was going for singing classes.'

Realisation slowly dawned on Joseph. He had been barking up the wrong tree in the wrong forest all along. With some difficulty, he found speech.

'So the grey skirt was just a coincidence... A red herring. A garden path.'

'Yup.'

Joseph reeled from this revelation. No wonder he couldn't quite remember where he had been going that morning. He wasn't on his way to college. He was probably going for a movie or something.

Utpal stopped and put the bike on its side stand. 'Just a minute, please,' he said to Aastha.

Then he grabbed Joseph's neck, shook it slowly and said, 'You bloody cheap duplicate version of Sherlock Holmes, you mad Einstein, you Suppandi-who-thinks-he's-Hercule-Poirot, you dragged me along on a wild goose chase of 400 grey-skirted girls. And all this time she was from Handique. Where girls don't even wear skirts!'

Joseph didn't have a decent reply. 'That's why I didn't have a bag on me,' he said, more to himself than to the others.

'You don't need a bag,' said Utpal, still mock-strangling him. 'You need a straitjacket!'

'Well, at least you found a girlfriend!'

Utpal let go. 'Well, you said the magic words. For that, I'm letting go, otherwise our next stop would have been MMC Hospital. *You* push now.'

Joseph took hold of the bike and heaved, still in a slight daze over the wild-goose chase.

'Handique,' he said, as if it was some weird-tasting overrated exotic food which he couldn't bring himself to swallow.

'Grey skirt... Grey skirt my ass!' said Utpal and kicked Joseph on the arse.

'Ow!' yelled Joseph. 'Asshole!'

'A second of which is exactly what you need right now. Sorry about the violence,' said Utpal to Aastha, 'but I really needed some catharsis. You don't know how much this idiot dragged me around skirt-chasing.'

As they walked to the restaurant, they told each other brief histories of themselves. Aastha had studied Sociology at Handique Girls' College and law at the Gauhati University, then left for Hyderabad to work for a corporate law firm shortly after her cancelled wedding. Her father was a senior officer at All-India Radio, and taught singing because it was his passion.

'So are you here on leave?' asked Joseph.

'No, I quit.'

'Why? Didn't like the food?'

'No, not that.' Aastha paused for a couple of seconds before answering. 'Papa was lonely.'

'That's all?'

'I mean, he never said so, but I always noticed how very crushed he used to look whenever we parted at the airport.'

Joseph suspected there was more than Aastha was letting on, but it was their first meeting, so he didn't expect her to share all her secrets right away.

'Your mother?'

'Passed away when I was two. Don't really remember her.'

'Sorry to hear that. What had happened?'

'Cerebral malaria.'

The day being a Sunday, Pirish was closed, so they had their momos at Momo Ghar, which was just around the corner. To both Utpal and Joseph's amazement, Aastha dunked eleven momos!

'Mein Gott!' said Utpal. 'The most I've seen a girl eat is seven. How many is that—eleven?'

'Sh—bad manners,' said Joseph.

'This happens whenever I have to sing in public,' said Aastha. 'Before the performance, I can't eat anything, and when it's done, whether good or bad, I get some kind of high and feel disproportionately hungry.'

'Aren't you worried about putting on weight?' said Utpal.

'Not really. I don't smoke, don't drink, so this is one of my few indulgences.'

'So what d'you think?' said Joseph as they drank coffee. 'Could we—see each other? At least to find out if we're compatible.'

Aastha mulled over the question for a second, then said, 'I don't know. State your case.'

'Well—ahem... In a nutshell—I've come to believe that relationships are most probably predestined. No amount of effort or adjustment will work if the relationship isn't already meant to be—destined to be, if you like—unless both the parties are true soulmates—the made-for-each-other types. And I think the fact that I didn't even speak to you but I still remembered you for nine years of my life means something. Maybe it was some kind of sign from the powers above. Fate, destiny, whatever. Maybe that's why your wedding—excuse my saying this—fell through at the last minute. Maybe because you were actually destined to be with someone else. It might be me, it might not. But I say, why don't we try to find out?'

'Good speech,' said Utpal after a second's quiet.

'Yes, good speech,' said Aastha. 'The main problem is—I don't believe in the made-for-each-other concept. What I believe is that irrespective of whether you've known someone for ten years or ten minutes, once you get together, you have to work every day at keeping it together. Doesn't matter whether you had zero chemistry at the beginning or hundred.'

Joseph smiled and said, 'We did have one hundred per cent chemistry for a minute in 2002, didn't we?'

'I don't know, Joseph. I don't know.'

As they exited Momo Ghar and pushed the bike the last few metres to the petrol pump, Joseph said, 'Look, let's not rush into a verdict either way. Let's meet a few times, see if things work out. What say?'

Aastha thought about it and said, 'Let me think about it. Give me your number. I'll call you.'

Aastha saved Joseph's number while Utpal replenished the dehydrated bike's reserves.

'One question,' said Aastha. 'What if we don't turn out to be soulmates? What if you yourself start feeling that way?'

'Well... I don't know. I'd never considered that possibility.'

'Hm. You're quite a case of positive thinking.'

Utpal started the bike and brought it over, then dismounted. 'So where d'you live?' he said.

'Chandmari Colony.'

'Well, we're practically neighbours then. Go, drop her.'

'What about you?' asked Joseph.

'I'll walk. You can pick me up after you've dropped her.'

'Um, are the brakes okay?' asked Aastha.

Joseph raised an eyebrow and asked, 'Why?'

'Let me do the driving.'

'Eh?'

'Don't panic. I used to ride my dad's bike before he finally bought a car.'

Joseph and Utpal looked at each other doubtfully.

'In fact,' said Aastha, 'you don't have to dump Utpal for me. You two sit behind. I'll drive.'

'What!' said the two together.

'Have you two composed a song where the chorus goes "What!"? I said I'll drive and you two sit.'

'Tripling?' said Utpal. 'Are you kidding?'

'No I'm not. Don't look so sceptical. I once took a 110-kg aunty to hospital.'

'You mean your trip ended in taking her to hospital or—' said Joseph.

'No, stupid,' said Aastha, punching his arm. 'Her mother had been admitted there and there was no one else to take her that night.'

'The brakes are fine, but I don't think it's such a good idea. And there'll be cops.'

'Only on the main road. We'll go this way.'

Joseph still looked doubtful. Utpal was trying to telepathically tell Joseph, 'Dude, one girl sold your first bike. Make sure this isn't the girl that crashes your second.'

'Are you absolutely sure?' said Joseph.

'Yessir, I am.'

'Okay, but if things get hairy, we switch.'

'Fine.'

Utpal wasn't too excited about the idea. 'Why don't the two of you go? I'll walk.'

Aastha said, 'Don't look so worried. Just get on and hang on.'

Aastha mounted. Joseph took his place behind her. Utpal, to his extreme trepidation and against his better judgement, squeezed in behind Joseph.

'Try not to stick too close,' said Joseph.

'Mokkel, there are three of us on a bike meant for a maximum of two. What d'you expect?'

Aastha kickstarted the bike. Joseph gulped. Utpal thought of his mother.

A slight wobble gave both the boys teensy heart attacks, but as soon as Aastha had switched to second gear, the ride became smooth. She exhibited remarkable control for a girl with two boys on the same bike.

She turned into Ambari, entered a small side lane, exited outside St Mary's School, then took the road beside the HDFC office at Senikuthi.

'Well, you're not bad at all,' said Joseph.

'Thank you.'

'Dude,' whispered Utpal in Joseph's ear, 'd'you want me to push you closer to her?'

'Bugger off! What d'you think this is—a bikeborne threesome?'

'Bugger is the right word.'

'Shut up and keep a respectable distance.'

Just after the pretty Nabagrah war cemetery, the road veered up dramatically.

Joseph said, 'Er, Aastha, are you sure you'll be able to take us up that?'

'Let's find out.'

Before Joseph could make any further suggestions, Aastha accelerated and tore up the incline. Unfortunately, the incline was just too much for any bike to bear the burden of three people. Aastha came down to first gear, but the bike was at its limits. It came to a stop halfway to the crest and started teetering.

'Ho whoa whoa get off!' said Joseph to Utpal. 'Quick! Off!'

Utpal hurriedly dismounted and grabbed the bike just before they completely lost balance.

'Whew. Close one,' he said.

'Sorry, guys,' said Aastha.

'Not your fault, really,' said Joseph. 'No one would've made it with three fellows riding.'

Aastha rode the bike alone to the top of the slope and waited for them to catch up.

'Shall I take over?' said Joseph, looking at the descent, which was as steep as the ascent.

'This is the part for which I asked whether the brakes are okay,' said Aastha.

'Oh. They're fine, but I don't know whether I'd risk our necks on them.'

'The two of you go. I'll walk,' said Utpal.

Aastha didn't insist this time, so she and Joseph mounted the bike.

Joseph said to Utpal, 'If anything happens, tell Mom and Dad that I died for women's lib.'

'Shut up, stupid,' said Aastha. 'Nothing's gonna happen. This is my favourite shortcut.'

'Mine too,' said Joseph. 'How come we never crashed into each other?'

Joseph's imagination made the descent more harrowing than it actually was. The most worrying possibility in his mind was that they'd overshoot a curve in the slope and plummet into the well in the compound below. Fortunately, nothing untoward happened. Aastha used the brakes well, and it was an uneventful downhill ride upto the temple, where she stopped and waited for Utpal to catch up.

The three of them negotiated a few more lanes, drawing eyes everywhere, and finally landed up in front of a compound with a small house, a flower garden and a big vegetable patch.

'Here we are,' said Aastha as they dismounted.

'So I guess it's bye for now,' said Joseph.

'Yup.'

'Bye,' said Utpal. 'It was nice to finally meet you. And if I ever need to be taken to hospital, I'll call you.'

Aastha smiled. 'So, Joseph, like I said, let me think things over, and I'll call you.'

'Right-o... Bye then.'

Joseph and Utpal drove off while Aastha stood at the gate and waved goodbye. She was smiling, but Joseph couldn't gauge the nature of the smile.

'Dude,' said Utpal, 'she didn't give you her number'.

'No, but she'll call.'

'How d'you know? And how do we know that was her real house? Maybe she lives somewhere else and just got off there to throw you off track.'

'You're paranoid.'

Chapter 11

Don't think of Elephants

Joseph couldn't sleep till 2 am. Had he already fallen in love? He was afraid to, yet he was afraid that he had, and it had happened in the following three steps:

1. When he heard her singing
2. When she said 'No, stupid' and punched his arm
3. Her bike-riding

But what if Aastha refused to even be friends? That was an eventuality too terrible to even consider. To keep his mind off her, he had watched three films on the trot—*Shaun of The Dead*, *Unforgiven*, and *Sympathy For Lady Vengeance*. No romance of the day. Although his head was pretty much groggy by the end of *Lady Vengeance*.

He also kept his phone on his person all the time, even when he went to the bathroom. The next morning, he was lucky to catch it when it slipped out of his hands and nearly fell into the commode.

At around 11 am, when he had started practising speed-picking exercises, the phone finally rang. It was a new number.

'Hello?' said Joseph, an unsaid prayer on his lips.

'Hello, sir,' said a cheerful female voice. 'We have a new caller plan which also gives you insurance against mobile theft.'

Damn. It wasn't her. 'Uh, what kind of insurance is that?'

'Well, sir, if your mobile gets stolen you can claim upto 50 per cent of its retail price, minus the number of percentage points in years that it's been in use, but not inflation-adjusted.'

'What?'

'The only condition is that you'll have to prove that the phone was stolen and not lost by you.'

'Wh-what? How on earth is anyone supposed to do that? Get a certificate of theft from the thief?'

'You, sir, are an impolite nitwit.'

'What! Who is this? Aastha, that you?'

'Would you like to meet at the Panbazar Baptist Church once more and find out?' said Aastha in her normal tone.

'Oh, it's you,' said Joseph, and burst into a relieved laugh. 'I was wondering which telemarketeer would use such a Victorian construct. "You, sir, are an impolite nitwit".'

'So how've you been?'
'I'd be lying if I said fine.'
'Why?'
'I've been waiting for your call.'
'Let me get to the point straightaway so that you don't get your hopes up. I have some terms and conditions if we're gonna be friends. Can we meet and discuss them?'
'Great. Sure.'
'But the first one I need to tell you right now. Don't even think of falling in love with me.'
'You're not lesbian, are you?'
Aastha laughed. 'No. Why?'
'That was quite a blanket declaration to make. "Don't even *think* of falling in love with me." A girl being able to ride a bike as well as a guy isn't a big deal, but it's not a good sign on those lines either. And maybe that's the real reason you backed out of your wedding at the last minute, because you had an epiphany about your orientation, and you told us the dowry story as a good cover.'
Aastha laughed again and said, 'No, stupid. I'm not a lesbian. I'm only telling you this for your own good.'
'How? Or why?'
'I'll tell you when the time's right. So, shall we meet?'
'Sure. Shall I pick you up?'
'No need. I'm already nearby.'

'Okay, then I'll be there in twenty-five.'

Joseph made a mad dash for his best T-shirt and jeans.

Half an hour later, he was seated with Aastha on a metal bench next to the pretty church graveyard.

'So what are the terms and conditions? And the fine print?'

'Actually, the only condition is the one I've already told you. The rest aren't conditions—they're tasks.'

'Tasks? *The Twelve Tasks of Asterix*?'

'The four tasks of Joseph. By performing them, you'll be hanging out with me,' said Aastha with a hint of playful flirtation.

'Oho. I'm privileged.'

'Shut up. As long as you remember not to fall in love.'

'Are you absolutely sure you're not a lesbian?'

'For the nth time, yes I'm sure.'

'Prove it.'

Aastha laughed and said, 'What d'you want me to do, rip off your clothes and do something to you here in public?'

Joseph let off a burst of staccato laughter and said, 'Okay, I won't bring it up again—for some time at least. But—what if *you* fall in love with me first?'

'We'll see about that when—and if—it happens... The deal is loaded in my favour, to be honest. But, if at any time you feel I'm taking undue advantage of you, you're free to go.'

'Well, what are the four tasks?'

'I'll tell you the first two first. Numero uno—I want to sing with a band at a decent-size concert.'

'That's fantastic! That's the exact same thing I've been thinking of! You sing, I play guitar, Utpal drums—great! IIT's Alcheringa is coming up. We'll play there.'

'That sounds good.'

'Great!' said Joseph with a very wide smile splitting his face. 'What's next?'

'I want you to help me find a nice wife for my dad.'

'Eh?' said Joseph, with the very wide smile splitting his face suddenly vanishing. 'That's—that's the exact same thing I haven't been thinking of.'

'Too tough?'

'No—no,' said Joseph, making a quick recovery. 'But—but why?'

'Well, I can't live with him forever, can I? There's marriage and things. I don't want him to be lonely without me around.'

'Noble thought. I think the percentage of girls who actually want a stepmom is less than 0.000001.'

'I don't want a stepmom. I want my dad to have a wife.'

'Hm, yes. That's what I meant.'

'So you're okay with it?'

'Yeah, sure.'

'You don't sound so sure.'

'Better be underconfident than over.'

'That's true. So how'll we do it?'

'Well... we harnessed the power of the worldwide web to find you, so I'm sure we can use it again to find a suitable girl for your dad.'

'Please say "woman" instead of "girl".'

'Oops. You're right. I just meant it in the conventional bride-hunting sense.'

'I know. So we should register Papa's profile on marriage websites?'

'I guess that's the most obvious way.'

'Very good. Let's do it,' said Aastha, standing up.

'Right now?'

'Yes, right now. Why delay?'

As they walked to the bike, Joseph asked, 'One question. What if, despite my best efforts to the contrary, I do end up falling in love with you?'

Aastha searched the church grounds for an answer, then said, 'I don't know, Joseph, I don't know. Just don't let me know, I suppose. Or at least don't expect me to reciprocate.' Then she scoffed and said, 'God, I feel like I'm just going to be using you.'

'That's okay. I'm used to being used.'

Aastha smiled and said, 'I'll try to use you less.'

'I'm not that useless.'

'Enough with the puns. Let's go.'

Off they went to Moon Internet Café, where they registered Mr Mishra's profile on three marriage sites and uploaded a couple of pictures of him taken from Aastha's Facebook account.

'Your dad still looks like a '70s film hero,' said Joseph as he clicked on 'Register'.

'Hope we find him a Hema Malini.'

Over cups of machine-made coffee opposite Guwahati Commerce College, Joseph and Aastha found they had far too much in common to be in safe won't-fall-in-love territory. They loved comics,' 90s music, Korean films and cooking, they didn't have too much respect for people who didn't know lose from loose, nurtured a healthy disdain for people who used the apostrophe to denote plurals, and reserved utter contempt for those who wrote 'hwz lyf'.

'And then they'll say it's okay as long as you understand the meaning,' said Aastha.

'I guess that argument may be just a wee bit valid.'

'Well, it gets my goat. Should Michaelangelo have stopped about halfway and said, "Well it's okay as long as you understand that this statue is of David... Although the genital area may seem slightly androgynous."'

Joseph laughed and fell in love some more. He had a thing for this increasingly endangered species—girls skilled with words, no matter in which language.

Aastha noticed the look in his eyes, but she ignored it and tried to change his train of thought.

'So, Joseph, are there any terms and conditions that *you* would like to lay down? It's only fair.'

'Wellll...' said Joseph, scratching his head. 'I don't know how we're placed relationship-wise, but if you were my girlfriend, and I know you're not, I'd say the one thing I hate most are secrets and lies.'

'That's two things.'

'Yeah, but one usually implies the other.'

'Not necessarily. Anyway, never mind. I get your point.'

'Yup. I wouldn't want you to keep any secrets from me—no matter how terrible.'

'Even if it was that I got seduced by some other guy and slept with him?'

'Well... yeah.'

'Hmmm...'

'That was the most dangerously loaded "hmmm" I've heard in my life.'

Aastha giggled and said, 'Let's see what happens. When's Alcheringa, by the way?'

'End of January, I think. We have a month to practise.'

'Are we going in with another guitar or keyboard?'

'Guitar. Utpal's cousin Nabajit.'

'Okay. And who does bass?'

'That's something I need to sort out. Will you come home with me now, so we can sort out the set list and also try out a few songs?'

Aastha looked at Joseph, smiled, and said, 'Do I know you well enough?'

'You know I won't try any funny business. And even if I do, you can always kick me between the legs and run.'

'Why bother kicking? All that's needed is to reach down and squeeze. I do it all the time.'

'All the time?'

'Okay, twice. Once here. Once in Delhi. I punched the horny middle-aged man of Delhi on the nose too.'

'Splendid. I prefer my precious family jewels in one piece each, so you can rest assured that you'll be unmolested at my place.'

'Okay,' said Aastha with that fanged smile of hers which Joseph was beginning to find so irresistible.

Joseph had picked up just a handful of female songs on the guitar. One of them was *Runaway* by The Corrs. By the time Aastha had finished singing it in all her note-perfect glory, he knew was well and truly hooked. There was no way he could help falling in love with her, except if she too did something really down and dirty like drugging him and stealing his bike and selling it off.

'I love the flattened fifth note on the violin at the end,' said Aastha.

'Yeah, I love y—it,' said Joseph.

Aastha sang him one of her original songs. Joseph liked it immediately. She hadn't set it to music yet, so Joseph suggested they put together the chord progression. It was in E flat, so he recommended that they do it in E instead. That way, it'd be easier to play and would sound nicer with some open strings.

Late in the afternoon, he dropped her back at the same place. This time, her father's car was parked in its shed.

'So this *is* your place?' he said.

'Any doubt?'

'Utpal thought you might have been trying to throw us off the trail.'

'He's sweet.'

As he drove away, Joseph knew he was definitely done for.

Chapter 12

Swallowing Pride and Dough

Joseph rang the doorbell. Utpal was beside him. Neither of them was too comfortable with the possible paths that the upcoming conversation might take.

The door was opened by Rituraj himself, and to say he was pleased to see Joseph would be a gross distortion of the truth.

'You? What d'you want?' said Rituraj. Then he said to Utpal, 'Why didn't you tell me you were bringing him along? I could've gone somewhere else. Like hell.'

'C'mon man, don't start like that,' said Utpal. 'It's childish.'

'I don't care. I mean—what's this—a trick visit? You can come in, and *you* can piss off.'

'Look—' started Joseph, getting just a little hot under the collar.

'Stop talking like a kid,' said Utpal to Rituraj.

'I don't care whether I'm talking like a kid or like the oldest man in Japan. He's not welcome.'

'Aunty!' called out Utpal in a mock complaining voice.

'You don't have to drag Ma into this,' said Rituraj.

'Aunty!' said Utpal again.

'Utpal, that you?' said Rituraj's mother's voice. It came not from inside the house, but from the terrace, the staircase to which was on their right side.

'Yes, Aunty,' said Utpal, still in the complaining-little-kid tone. 'Ritu isn't letting us in.'

'Let them in, son,' said Ritu's mother.

'Heard that?' said Utpal triumphantly. 'Let us in.'

'You can come in. Not him.'

Joseph said, close to flying off the handle, 'It's not *your* house, is it? It's your mom and dad's house, and she said let them in, so I'm coming in.'

'What for? You wanna play *Rock On—Rock On*?'

Joseph tried to step in, but Ritu pushed him out. 'No you're not coming in.'

'Oh yes I am. What're you gonna do?'

And a brief but very funny standup wrestling match ensued, with Joseph trying to force his way in the door and Ritu jostling to keep him out.

'What the hell are you two babies doing!' said Utpal. 'Aunty! They're fighting!'

'What!' said Aunty's voice, this time concerned. She came down the stairs, a basket of sunned flour in her hands. In the melee, the two wrestlers ended up giving Utpal a hard shove backward. He tripped on the last stair and landed on his substantial bottom, which saved him from much damage, but his flailing hands connected with the flour basket and floomp! The next second, the flour was all over his head and shoulders and he looked like the abominable doughman. Or flourman.

Joseph and Ritu terminated their wrestling match.

'Oh my God!' exclaimed Ritu's mother. 'I am *so* sorry, Utpal. So sorry.'

'It's not your fault, Aunty,' said Utpal very calmly, spitting out a bit of flour. His eyes and mouth formed three small circles of black and brown in the shapeless white mass his head presently was. 'It's these two mokkels!' he yelled. 'Stupid jackasses! Do I need to remind you that we're twenty-seven years old! Fighting like Calvin and Hobbes. Now shut up! Not another word! Let's all go in quietly or I'll personally rip both your pairs of arses off.'

'Sorry,' said Ritu and Joseph together, chastised.

'Shut up and move.'

'Let's get you cleaned up,' said Ritu's mother.

Five minutes later, Utpal was in the bathroom washing the dough off. Ritu and Joseph were sitting in the hall, a sullen silence occupying the space of easy conversation.

Ritu broke the ice. 'Sorry.'

'Actually,' said Joseph, 'I came to say sorry myself.'

'For?'

'You know—for all the things I said.'

'Do you even remember all the things you said?'

'I'm not too sure.'

'You called me a talentless good-for-nothing who'd never be able to do anything in life.'

'Oh.'

'And that forget about playing bass, I probably couldn't even play with myself correctly.'

'Oh.' Joseph was highly embarrassed that he could have made such ungentlemanly remarks about his buddy.

'And that I should marry some fat rich family girl and then have babies with dyslexia.'

'Come on, I couldn't have said that.'

'But you did.'

'No I didn't.'

'Yes you did.'

Utpal's voice shot in through the bathroom door. He said, 'I can hear rising voices. If you two start again, I'm gonna come out and beat the crap out of you two even if I'm naked, and then I'll make you eat all this dough I'm washing off.'

The two squabblers quietened down.

'You did,' whispered Ritu sharply.

Joseph realised this was a bitter truth he had to swallow. 'Shit. That's really bad. I'm sorry. I was really angry that you were leaving.'

'Are you sorry about saying the other things as well?'

'Yes, of course I am. I'm real sorry... I know this is going to sound selfish, but I've come for a very specific reason.'

'Where d'you wanna play?' said Ritu with a knowing smile. 'Alcheringa?'

'Yup.'

'There's not even a month left. How are we going to get to the finals, forget about winning?'

'It's not about winning this time.'

'Then? And we certainly can't do anything without a good vocalist.'

'Yeah. I know I suck.'

'And he sucks only just a little less than you,' said Ritu, pointing in the direction of the bathroom.

'I heard that,' said Utpal.

'We've found a vocalist,' said Joseph.

'Who?'

'Aastha.'

'The Aastha channel?'

'Aastha Mishra.'

'A girl?'

'Yeah.'

'Forget it. No. No way. And someone named Aastha Mishra sounds like she could lead the bhajan group at the temple, not a rock band at Alcheringa.'

'That's the most illogical argument I've heard. All you need to do is listen to her once. This is how the scene will go: she'll start singing, you'll start listening, we'll crane down and dolly around her, your mouth will drop wide open at the power in her voice, and then you'll be speechless and you'll just nod yes, we'll do it. Just take my word for it, she's good.'

'As good as Tipriti?'

'Maybe. I don't know what Tipriti sounds like singing ballads, so can't really compare.'

'How'd you find her? Wait—is this your bus stop girl?'

'Yeah.'

'Holy shit. This is unreal. You actually found her? And she's a singer?'

'Oh yes sir.'

'Man, that's something. Practically a sign from the gods.'

Joseph nodded happily.

'Y'know what,' said Ritu in flashback mode, 'I haven't touched the bass since that day'.

'I'm sorry, mate. Really.'

'Fine, man. No need to be dramatic. I think what you said hurt even more because deep down inside, I knew it was true.'

'Oh, come on.'

'No, look, once the anger had subsided, I took a good look at myself. All these movies and songs say stuff like follow your dreams, follow your heart—highly overrated concepts, if you ask me. There's no point following your dreams if you're not good enough—look at all those besura weirdos on *Indian Idol* and other shows—even they're following their "dreams".'

'But you play decent.'

'Decent is correct. Decent enough to accompany you for most songs. But great? That I realised I definitely am not. You could give me two extra fingers on each hand and I'd still be not even the dust on John Myung's or Steve Harris's boots. I realised that I make a better engineer than bassist.'

'You'd be great if you practised.'

'Perhaps. But I guess I didn't want to put in that much hard work. The burn isn't as strong in me as it is in you.'

Joseph knew Ritu was right. 'I suppose that's something I should've understood back then.'

Utpal had suddenly materialised before them. 'Band of brothers again, eh? Good.'

His remark was completely drowned out by the loudness of the technicolour shirt he was wearing. Not only were its colours competing to blind innocent passers-by, the shirt itself was far too tight for Utpal, and it was almost literally bursting at the seams. One heavy meal would do the trick.

'Which time machine did you steal that from?' said Joseph.

'It's his,' said Utpal. He asked Ritu, 'What? You wanna go back to the technicolour psychedelic '70s? Were you drunk and colour-blind when you bought this?'

'I never wear that,' said Ritu, pointing behind Utpal. 'It was Ma's choice.'

Utpal turned and saw Ritu's mother standing just behind him. 'Er—uh—oh—Aunty, I meant—it's too tight for me.'

'That's obvious,' said Ritu's ma. 'He's not healthy like you.' From her smile, it seemed like she had probably missed the gist of Utpal's disparaging remarks.

'He's not "healthy",' said Ritu. 'He's fat.'

'Shut up, roll number 111,' said Utpal. Ritu's roll number in Cotton College was considered by one and all to be thoroughly befitting of his figure.

Chapter 13

Freezing Fingers & More

Twenty-eight days later, Aastha, Joseph, Ritu, Utpal and Utpal's cousin Nabajit the guitarist, stuffed themselves into Aastha's dad's WagonR and drove to IIT Guwahati.

They had diligently practised eight songs, only two of which were covers, songs which all of them loved—Evanescence's *My Immortal* and Colbie Caillat's *Fallin' For You*. Of the others, two were Aastha's compositions, two Joseph's and one each were Ritu's and Nabajit's. They had decided to call themselves The AM Band, after Aastha's initials. No dark or deathly or demonic names—they found them juvenile now.

The drive through the 1800-acre campus was more picturesque during daylight, since one could see the lush green hills in the distance. A light mist was beginning to form and it was bloody cold.

A stage and marquee had been erected for the event, which was named Rockophonix. Assam Engineering

College, which was practically around the corner, and IIT Guwahati seemed to try to outdo each other every year in organising the bigger and better rock event, starting with the name—AEC's rock contest was called Pyrokinesis. Not to be outdone, Guwahati Medical College called its rock event Pye-rock-xia.

Nabajit had been among the three students in charge of organising Pyrokinesis that year, and he had pulled off a remarkable coup by bringing over the Pakistani band Jal to perform at AEC. Needless to say, it was a heavily attended event.

Aastha had only had a light lunch, as was her wont on concert days. As for Joseph's appetite—rain, storm, government overthrows, cricket losses, failed exams—nothing could interfere with it, and he had ensured that they had brought along enough momos and rolls to have a proper dinner. Their turn could arrive as late as midnight.

They waited in one of the rooms allotted to the bands while Nabajit went and completed the formalities. He came back with a black look on his face.

'We're last,' he announced.

'What!' said Joseph and Utpal.

'There's that chorus again,' said Aastha.

'You're kidding,' said Ritu.

'No. We *are* last.'

'Crap! No!' said Utpal. 'How many bands are there?'

'Eighteen.'

'Eighteen! Holy crap! At twenty minutes each, that's three and a half hours, which means one o' clock! Shit!'

'That's *if* they start on time,' said Joseph.

'Shit! Shit shitty shittety shit!'

'Stop saying it before you actually feel like it,' said Joseph. 'How did they order the bands anyway? In decreasing order of distance to campus?'

'Lottery,' said Nabajit.

'Were you there?'

'No. He said I just missed it.'

'I smell fish.'

'Wait a minute,' said Utpal to Nabajit. 'Does this have anything to do with stealing Jal from under their noses?'

'I think so,' said Nabajit with a wicked grin. 'In fact, it *is* so, heh heh.'

'What's the back story here?' said Aastha.

'Well, Jal was supposed to perform at IIT this year. But I played a bit of dirty politics and got them to come to AEC instead.' Nabajit couldn't help a conceited laugh. 'This guy Mohit—he's taking revenge on me.'

'You're laughing, mokkel?' said Ritu. 'We'll be playing at midnight. Our fingers will be frozen stiff!'

Nabajit only laughed a bit more. Utpal's reply was to kick him in the arse.

Ritu was wrong. They didn't play at midnight. They played at 2 am. Justifying their band name in the process. But Ritu was also right. Their fingers were frozen stiff by that time.

The guitarists rubbed their palms and fingers together vigorously to get back some warmth and limberness.

'Asshole, look what you've done,' said Ritu to Nabajit.

'I just hope,' said Joseph, 'that they don't ask us to play *Mon Maya* first. I'm a little worried about doing the solo.'

'Would you please play your original song, *Mon Maya*, first?' said Ambar Das, one of the three judges, when they were up on stage and had finished their soundcheck.

Before that, as they were plugging in their gear, Aastha's appearance had caused quite a stir. Bands fronted by girls are a rare breed, and the rare sighting of an example of the species was received with even more raucous enthusiasm in an institution where the sex ratio was one girl to three million boys.

'Oye female vocalist!' yelled someone in the crowd.

'Hi sexy babe!'

'Sing *Piya Tu Ab Toh Aaja*.'

Aastha was unruffled, but Joseph wasn't too pleased about the heckling.

Once she began singing, though, the crowd fell in line. *Mon Maya* was catchy and peppy, just the kind of song to get a crowd up on its feet.

Unfortunately, Joseph's worries about his frozen fingers being able to play the fast part of the solo turned out to be well founded. One bar ended up being off-tempo gibberish, and he ended up hitting a very bad wrong note as well—the komal *Re*.

Some redemption was provided by Aastha's alaap after the solo, and the last chorus and outro solo went by without error. The song ended to cheers and applause.

'Yeah baby!'

'Sexy babe sexy singing!'

Joseph wanted to bring his guitar down plonk on the heckler's skull, but he told himself that these things were par for the course. The chief heckler was an overweight semi-sloshed dude with specs and a four-day stubble.

They ended up playing an all-original set. Whether it was the really late hour or the cold or a combination of the two, they unfortunately ended up making a few more mistakes. Utpal forgot to stop playing during a brief drumless interlude, Ritu played two bars of a middle eight bassline when he should have been playing the final chorus and Nabajit's second string was distuned throughout the final song. Aastha was the only one who survived unscathed, and it was primarily for her that the vigorous applause was as they finished their set.

'Well done sexy babe!' yelled the semi-sloshed dude as they got off the stage.

Joseph blew a fuse. 'Teri ma hogi sexy babe!'
'Oye! Teri toh!'
'Aaja saale!'

The semi-sloshed dude tried to come towards Joseph, but his friends held him back.

'It's okay,' said Aastha to Joseph. 'No big deal.'

'Hey, AM Band!' called out a voice. It was Ambar Das. He was stretching his limbs and walking over to them.

'You sing really, really well,' he said to Aastha.

'Thanks.'

Ordinarily, Joseph would've thought here was another bloke-in-a-puny-position-of-power who was just trying to chat up a pretty girl, but Ambar had a reputation for being a man of class and integrity. He was primarily a drummer, known for easily picking up and playing odd-time beats as accurately as a metronome, but was also very good with a guitar, and his knowledge of music was vast.

'I really liked your songs,' he said. 'Almost no one composes stuff with melody these days. If only you had been tighter, you'd have been sure to be through.'

The boys gloomily nodded.

'It's hard to play this late,' said Ritu. 'Bloody cold.'

'I know,' said Ambar. 'It's happened to me too. Keep your fingers warm before playing next time. Wear gloves.'

Then he said to Aastha, 'I know I'm not supposed to say this now, but I think you deserve to be told that you're easily the best vocalist out of everyone here. Not a single note flat. And everything on tempo. Really, really good. You have a great future if you do this professionally.'

'Thanks a lot, Ambar da.'

'Ciao, then. I need to get back and total up the scores.'

As Ambar Das went back to the judges' desk, Mohit, one of the three IITians in charge of the event, and in particular, the one responsible for them playing last, came up to Aastha and said, 'Hi. Can I please take a picture with you?'

Aastha said, 'With the whole band.'

'Okay.'

They posed with Mohit and several other students who had also become fans of Aastha. Later, whenever Mohit uploaded those pictures, he made sure to crop Nabajit's face out of the frame.

'I think you'll become really famous one day,' he said to Aastha. 'I'm taking these pictures in advance so I can show off later.'

Aastha smiled gracefully and said, 'That's nice of you.'

Joseph was delighted at all the adulation the object of his affection was receiving. He knew they had messed up, but she still shone out in the midst of the rubble.

Then he noticed she was quietly wiping away a tear.

'What's the tragedy?' said Joseph.

'Well, y'know—tears of joy,' said Aastha, trying to smile.

Joseph took a good look, then shook his head and said, 'You can tell me later, when the time's right.'

Aastha smiled genuinely this time. She probed Joseph's face for a moment, then made a decision.

'Let's go outside,' she said, and took his arm. Joseph looked at Aastha's hand. The only physical contact they had had until then consisted of her punches on his arm. He cast a glance at his buddies—they were smiling and giving him thumbs up. Utpal was air-smooching.

Aastha chose to sit on one side of a concrete culvert next to a small lake some distance away from the marquee. Half a moon provided just enough light to walk through the mist, which was on the verge of claiming to be fog as it went about covering the wide green fields.

'It's quiet here,' said Aastha.

'Yeah. Cold too. Wouldn't you rather sit in the car?'

'When I feel cold enough. Damn, I'm hungry. Would you get me my roll? And the chocolate. It's in my bag.'

'As you wish.'

Joseph went and came back with the chicken roll, the Dairy Milk Fruit & Nut and a bottle of water. Aastha hungrily wolfed down the roll without a word. Only after drinking some water did she find voice and let out a contented sigh.

'Aahhh, that was good,' she said as she unwrapped the chocolate and handed Joseph a couple of pieces.

'I've a secret to share. Big one.'

Joseph took a second before asking, 'What?'

'I'm dying.'

Aastha had said this without looking at Joseph. His first thought was to dismiss it as a painfully lame joke, then he quickly processed her tone in his head. It wasn't the over-serious tone one used when pulling a prank. It was more of a resigned 'Oh, dear' that one might say on finding out there's no more milk in the fridge. Nonetheless, he classified it as a pointless joke and just stared at her with a frown on his face.

Aastha noticed his funny expression and said, 'What?'

'I'm waiting for you to crack up,' said Joseph.

Aastha did crack up, but with a gallows laugh, and then said, 'I'm not kidding. I *am* dying. I have one of those very rare, incurable, terminal women's diseases. Von Brahm's syndrome.'

Joseph was still just staring without reacting, trying to fathom whether she was fooling around or being actually serious. Realising this, Aastha said: 'You wouldn't have heard of it. It's very very rare. Literally one in millions. Occurs in women of Mongoloid origin. Only one woman's lived beyond twenty-eight so far. Till thirty-two. And she spent her last years confined to bed.'

'How old are you?' said Joseph.

'Twenty-seven and counting.'

What rubbish. Joseph smirked. 'Shaadaap.'

Aastha smiled back and said, 'You don't believe me?'

'Of course I don't believe you. What crap. This is a bad joke with worse timing. Are you just trying to see how I'd react?'

'… I nearly died last year.'

'How? I mean what on earth happens with this disease I've never heard of?'

'Hurts like hell, for starters. I couldn't sleep for fifty-two straight hours…'

Aastha took out her cell and made a call.

'Who?' said Joseph.

Mr Mishra had been singing Ghulam Ali's *Le Chala Jaan* on his harmonium when he received Aastha's call.

'Yes beta, everything all right?'

'Yes, Papa. You're actually still awake?'

'Yes.'

'Well, don't worry. Everything's all right. We're done, and I'll be home in an hour.'

'Okay, that's good.'

'Listen, Papa… I've told Joseph about me.'

Mr Mishra's tone underwent a drastic change. He didn't get angry, but it was a cold jolt back to reality for him to have to discuss the one issue that he wished, by some miracle, he would never have to face.

'Everything?' he said.

'Yup, everything.'

Mr Mishra sighed. 'What was the need to?'

'I didn't want it to come as a sudden shock to him.' Then she looked at Joseph and said, 'And I didn't want him to fall in love with me.'

'Hm…'

'But he doesn't believe me. So would you please confirm it to him?'

'Is that really necessary?' said Mr Mishra, but Aastha was already pushing the phone against Joseph's unwilling ear.

'This is awkward,' he whispered to her. 'Hel-hello, Uncle.'

'Hello, Joseph.'

A few seconds passed while Joseph searched for the right words. 'Is—is it true?'

'Yes, it is.'

'There's—no cure?'

Joseph could hear Mr Mishra's breathing grow heavy as he said, 'No.'

'O—okay, Uncle. Good night.'

'Good night, beta.'

Joseph handed the phone back to Aastha, unseeing, speechless, dazed…

'This is why,' said Aastha, 'I didn't want you to fall in love with me. Why I want to find a companion for Papa.'

Joseph, still unable to look at Aastha, as if she was a dream and looking at her would cause him to wake up, opened his mouth, but no words came out.

Aastha said, 'This was one of my last wishes—to sing my own songs with a band of friends... Thanks for making it come true.'

Joseph could feel Aastha's eyes on him, but he still couldn't bear to make eye contact. As it was, he was finding it difficult to retain his composure.

Aastha let the enormity of the information sink in for a few seconds. Then she offered, 'Chocolate?'

Joseph finally looked at her, looked at the chocolate, then mechanically broke off a piece and popped it into his mouth. He looked around. The half moon was beautifully reflected in the black lake, and some of the brighter stars too. Far in the distance, a few students were returning to their hostels, one of them loudly singing a drunken version of the sutta song by Zeest—probably the same sloshed dude.

Aastha put a hand on Joseph's. He looked at it. This was the first unadulterated physical display of affection between them, although the glove on her hand was still a barrier. This would otherwise have been a moment of joy, but the preceding revelation had turned what should've been a beautiful event to remember into a most bittersweet one.

Still looking at Aastha's hand on his, Joseph said, 'You could have expected me to definitely not fall in love with you if you behaved like some arrogant, selfish, shallow bitch. But there's not one—iota—of any of these adjectives in you.'

Then he looked into her eyes and said, 'Did you really think I wouldn't fall in love with you?'

Aastha didn't reply. She didn't have to. They both knew the answer. Both of them knew they were one word away from breaking down, and were doing their best to put up a brave front and keep it together.

Aastha again broke into a smile. She exhaled sharply to control herself, then put the last piece of chocolate in her mouth and looked around for a place to throw the wrapper. There wasn't one, and she didn't want to dirty the lake, so she crumpled it up and put it into Joseph's jacket pocket.

She said, 'I used to have just two pieces at a time before.'

There were no words forthcoming from Joseph's lips, which were quivering. Suddenly realising this, he immediately tried to control his mouth into the formation of a stiff upper lip over a stiff lower lip.

Aastha removed the glove and offered her hand. Joseph took it. It felt warm against his own, which had suddenly gone extra cold.

They sat hand in hand in silence while the moon lazily shone on and the stars twinkled.

Chapter 14

Words that Draw Attention in Coffee Shops

Not surprisingly, they didn't qualify for the finals. A morose mood prevailed in the car as the five of them drove back to their places.

They reached home at 3.50. Under normal circumstances, Joseph would have been asleep by 3.52, but the lightning bolt that had hit him deprived him of sleep for another hour.

A week ago, he had dreamt that the sex ratio in the IITs had been inverted and he was playing not to an almost all-boys crowd, but to a rowdy throng of Filipinas, half of whom were speaking Dutch and the other half double-Dutch. Joseph was on stage, dressed in a suit made of faux Italian wool made in Bangladesh, but with no pants on! He remembered feeling thoroughly humiliated and wanting to get off stage and get some pants on first, but Utpal said to him, 'It's only for twenty minutes. You'll play more accurately if you don't wear pants. Richie Sambora said so.' When he started singing, and for some reason he was singing *Ding Dong Bell*, the girls started pelting him with an assortment of objects—old handkerchiefs, palak paneer, unpaid mobile bills, DermiCool talcum powder, water from Deepor Bil, a sexagesimal measuring tape, copied electrical engineering assignments, et cetera. The dream ended when one of the lady professors swore at him in Sanskrit, snatched a pickup truck and threw it in his face.

When Joseph woke at 9.30 the next morning—this morning, not the post-crazy-dream morning—the first thought that surged into his brain was that the notion of Aastha dying of an incurable disease had been just another ghastly nightmare. Almost immediately, reality rushed back in with memories of those few minutes last night that had turned his world upside down.

An hour later, he was Googling Von Brahm's Syndrome in Moon Internet Café. There was precious little information on the net regarding it. He came across a couple of study papers and journals, but the few pages he could read before Aastha arrived were too full of medical jargon for him to thoroughly understand—karyotypes, phenotypes, epidural and subarachnoid haemorrhage, polymerase chain reaction studies etc. One of the few terms he clearly understood was 'progressive central nervous and systemic organ failure'. Moon's watching saas-bahu serials at high volume didn't help his comprehension either. He quickly closed the windows before Aastha could see them.

'You haven't told anyone, have you?' she said.

'No.'

'Not even Utpal?'

'No.'

'Good. Don't tell. Anybody. And try to forget that you know. I don't want you behaving differently now.'

'I'll try,' said Joseph.

'Good,' said Aastha, and switched on her fanged smile. 'So, any prospective wives for Papa?'

They were checking out the matrimonial websites after almost a week, having been busy rehearsing earlier. The previous three weeks hadn't been too encouraging anyway, there being obviously not too many women in that age group. Of the three that had turned up in search results, one lived in Australia, one wanted a husband of her exact same caste and sub-caste and would also match kundalis before meeting—talk about picky—and the third had listed 'cing tv siriels' in her hobbies.

'She'd make a great match for Moon,' said Joseph. 'I probably could just pick up this computer and walk out of here and Moon would still be watching TV. They'd never get around to making babies. Five years later, somebody'd ask them about kids, and they'd say "Shit, we forgot".'

'What about rishta.com?'

Joseph checked. Nothing new there either.

'I think,' said Joseph, 'let's try the old-fashioned route. Through people we know. I'll ask my mother if she knows anyone.'

'Your mother?'

'Yeah. Matchmaking's her primary passion and occupation. She just happens to have a public sector job.'

'Okay. Ask her.'

'Our luck's in. She's on her way to Guwahati today.'

'How convenient.'

Later in the afternoon, Joseph and Aastha were seated with Joseph's mother at the Café Coffee Day near Commerce College.

Joseph's mother was used to seeing him with a variety of girls, but she was always polite and nice to all of them, and never asked her son when he was going to get serious and settle down. She took an instant liking to Aastha, who was at her most charming self with friends' mothers. Aastha found Joseph's mother's liveliness and enthusiasm a refreshing change from the usual cynicism of women that age.

'Five minutes after you called me I remembered the perfect match,' said Joseph's mother, taking out a photo. 'Babita Devi.'

Joseph reached for the photo but his mother held it back.

'Wait,' she said. 'Listen first. She used to work as a teacher. Husband was a contractor. Died two years ago of a heart attack. Two sons. One politician, one contractor. She moved in with them last year. In Dimapur now. Both sons are married with kids, but she's maintained herself quite well. Doesn't look like a grandma at all.'

'Lemme see,' said Joseph, reaching for the photo.

'Wait. Let me finish. She used to come to Aunty Purabi's house sometimes when we were in Tezpur. I really liked her. You were too young to remember, I suppose?'

'If you let me *see* her I might remember,' said Joseph through semi-gritted teeth. His mother's occasional eccentricities drove him bonkers.

'Anyway,' she said, still completely ignoring Joseph's outstretched hand, 'I talked to Purabi about Babita and she said that just last month she had called, and it seems she's really fed up because the grandkids are spoilt brats and she doesn't get along with her daughters-in-law.'

'Why?' said Joseph.

Their order arrived. Cappuccinos for mother and son, and a cold chocolate for Aastha, who grabbed it like Count Dracula would grab a teenage girl's neck. At least that was the comparison that struck Joseph's imagination.

'Why?' said his mother. 'That's because they're hopeless good-for-nothings who wanted to marry into rich families. All they care about is shopping and visiting beauty parlours.'

'Did Aunty Purabi say exactly that?' said Joseph, knowing his mother's highly developed skills at confidently getting details wrong and remembering conversations exactly the way they didn't happen.

'Maybe not… but I'm sure that's how they are.'

'Okay,' said a mildly exasperated Joseph. 'Can we see the photo now?'

His mother first tried to recall if there was anything more she had to add, then shook her head and finally gave them the photo.

If ever a photo made a good first impression, then this was it. Ma was right. Babita Devi didn't look like a grandma at all. She looked more like her kids had just finished college. The yellow saree she wore added to her air of elegance, but most importantly for Joseph, there seemed to be a sort of kindness and gentleness of spirit in her eyes.

'Well, what d'you think?' he asked Aastha.

'She looks nice. When can we meet her?'

'Well, you certainly can't go to her place in Dimapur and expect her sons to welcome you with open arms saying, "Please take our mother and get her married to some stranger".' It's better that you meet on neutral territory. The difficulty there also is—the sons are paranoid about security and kidnappings and all that, so they never let her go alone anywhere. At least a driver or bodyguard. But the good news is – at the moment, she's in Shillong. At her sister's place. Till Saturday. After that, it's back to Dimapur.'

'Hmm...' said Joseph.

In the following three seconds of silence, Joseph's mother's attention suddenly shifted to another recent topic of interest.

'Have you seen that hilarious new panty ad?' she said to Aastha. Then pulling apart imaginary panties in the air, she said loudly, "Is liye main bolti hoon footpath se panty mat khareedo!"'

'Ma! Sh!'

But the damage was already done. Words like 'panty', when spoken out loud in public places that are not women's undergarment shops, are bound to stab at people's ears and cause them to look in the direction of the speaker. The boy and the girl manning the counter and a couple at another table were all staring at Joseph's mother. She flashed them a big smile and cheerily said, 'Oh, sorry.'

'I'm not coming here for a year,' mumbled Joseph. Aastha only giggled.

'Here,' said Joseph's ma, taking out her cell, 'take Babita panty's number—I mean Aunty's number'.

Fortunately, this time it hadn't been loud, so mention of the p-word went by unnoticed.

'Was that deliberate?' said Joseph.

'I don't think so,' said his ma. She looked at Aastha and they shared a girl-bonding giggle.

Later, as Joseph walked his mother to her car, she said, 'I suppose I'll come again next month. Official training.' Then she looked back at Aastha, who was talking on her cell, and asked Joseph, 'How old is she?'

'My age.'

'I like her. Listen, I'm going to say this just once. Not to put pressure on you or anything but just as a matter of medical fact. You have three years if you want to secure yourself and start a family with her. I mean—it's healthy for the girl to have kids before she crosses thirty.'

Joseph let out a half-ironic chuckle. Before she crosses thirty. If.

'What?' said his mother. 'Don't tell me you're "just a friend" to her.'

'It's complicated.'

'Oh God. What does that mean? Never mind. I don't want to know. Tell me when you've figured it out. Look, she's a good girl. Don't let her get away. I can smell the good ones from a mile away.'

'Really?' said Joseph, mentally rolling up his sleeves. 'You liked Kaberi the most of all, whereas she was the one who boozed every other night and did drugs on weekends.'

'Okay, okay. I was wrong once.'

'Once? What about Monjuri?'

'Who Monjuri?'

'Oho. Selective memory? The one who you said was perfect for me because she was tall as well. And she turned out to be a high-class call girl.'

'Please let's not bring her up.'

'Back then, you were so eager for me to marry her. If I did, the right business for me to be in would've been a PCO.'

'Why?'

'Because I'd have several STDs.'

Ma didn't get the joke.

'I don't get the joke,' she said.

'STDs—y'know, like AIDS.'

'Shut up,' she said and slapped the back of his head.

On a hilltop smack in the middle of Guwahati is the Gandhi Mandap, which features a larger-than-life statue of the Mahatma and a memorial museum. One gets an almost-360-degree view of the city from here. Sunsets are especially beautiful to behold, and it was one such fiery sunset that tinged everything orange-red as Joseph called Babita Devi.

'Hello,' said a dignified voice. Joseph had turned the speaker on so Aastha too could hear.

'Babita Aunty, hi. It's Joseph here.'

'Joseph, hi hi hi hi. How are you doing? Your mother had called a little while ago.'

'I'm quite okay, Aunty. And you?'

'I'm good. My goodness, you were just a child when I last saw you. Now it feels like I'm talking to some young man I'm meeting for the first time.'

Joseph had a pleasant conversation with Babita Devi, obviously not letting on the real reason for calling.

The subject of lunch came up, and Joseph said he would be coming to Shillong with a friend the next day, so if she would be so kind—

'Of course of course,' she said. 'What would you like to eat? Pork, I guess?'

'Obviously, Aunty. Which idiot comes to Shillong and doesn't eat pork?'

Aastha whispered in Joseph's ear, 'Ask her if she can make momos?'

Joseph looked doubtful for a second, then asked.

'Well, I've never tried before,' said Babita Devi, 'but I'll make them for you. My sister makes them sometimes, so she'll know. Pork momos or chicken?'

'Oink oink,' said Joseph.

'I think she's nice,' said Aastha after the conversation had ended. She finally felt just a little optimistic about their chances. 'That was quick. Fancy that. The very first contact we get turns out to be such A-grade material. That was easy, don't you think?'

'Too easy. When life starts handing you things on a platter, it generally means there's a big bamboo right underneath waiting to shoved up somewhere where the sun don't shine as soon as your back's turned.'

Chapter 15

Going to Shillong

The aforementioned bamboo arrived that night in the form of a news report of some students' organisation calling for an Assam bandh the next day.

'You koopha,' said Aastha to Joseph on the phone. 'What do we do now?'

'We'll have to go,' said Joseph. 'Tomorrow's our only chance. Saturday she returns to Dimapur. And who knows when she'll be around again?'

'What if goondas throw stones at us?'

'Good things happen to me when you're around. So I don't think we'll run into them.'

'That's sweet of you, but what if we do?'

'We'll start early. Real early. Before any of those assholes wake up.'

'What if they wake up early as well?'

'If they *were* in the habit of waking up early, they'd have done something good with their lives by now.'

So Joseph landed up the next morning at 6.30 am at Aastha's place. It was foggy. And bloody cold. The sun was just starting to drag itself out of bed and open a pair of droopy eyelids to shed a little blue-grey light on the city.

Aastha had prepared hot chocolate to fuel their bodies and spirits till they crossed the state's border. Then they could breakfast at leisure in Nongpoh.

Joseph drove with headlights on, since the fog was moderately thick.

Unfortunately, at Khanapara, giving the lie to Joseph's optimism, there was a gang of six or seven young men standing on the road.

'Oh bloody hell,' said Aastha.

'These have to be the most dedicated goondas I've seen in my life. Troublemaking at seven on a cold winter morning.'

Joseph tried to avoid the goonda gang but they completely blocked the road and he had no choice but to stop. He would have preferred running two or three of them over and driving on, but a life in jail wasn't a career option he was too keen on.

The leader, a tall overweight man whose mouth was red from a lifetime of betel nuts and leaves, banged his hands on the bonnet before slapping Joseph's window.

'Open up,' he ordered.

Joseph rolled down his window.

'Where the hell d'you think you're going?'

'Er, we're going to Down Town Hospital,' said Joseph.

'Really? You've left it behind.'

'Eh? Oh, yeah.'

'What were going to do there? Sing songs to cheer up the patients?' said the leader, pointing to the guitar in the back seat. The other toughies laughed, more for effect than out of genuine mirth.

Leader goonda suddenly snatched the key out of the ignition.

'Hey, what're you doing?' said Joseph.

'Get out!'

Joseph and Aastha both got out of the car, tempers starting to rise.

Leader goonda said, 'It's Assam bandh today and you're trying to play lilimai with your girlfriend.'

'She's not my girlfriend,' said Joseph, while simultaneously wishing the statement were untrue.

Thwack! Leader goonda slapped Joseph.

'Then is she my girlfriend! Hold your ears and kneel down!'

Aastha came round between them and angrily said, 'What the hell is this! Who are you anyway, huh! Who d'you think you are?'

'Shut up girl. Don't make me slap you in the middle of the road.'

Joseph held Aastha back and said, 'Why're you threatening the girl? Talk to me. And the way you people keep doing this, I'm not surprised the rest of the country thinks we're a bunch of dangerous lazy good-for-nothings who just sit around and call for bandhs all day.'

Leader goonda was taken aback for a second by Joseph's brashness. Then he dangled Joseph's key before him and said, 'You're right. My eyes have opened. Go.'

Joseph knew this was only some kind of bait. All the same, he reached for the key, only for leader goonda to fling it away into the large drain on the side of the road. The goonda gang laughed.

'Dammit!' said Joseph, and scrambled downhill. The drain was at the bottom of a small slope of earth and grass, and the key had vanished somewhere out of sight.

'Bhaity Da,' said another of the goondas to the leader, 'there's another car coming'.

'Stop it,' said Bhaity Da.

The vehicle was a Tata Sumo. The thugs stood on the road and tried to wave it down, but the driver only braked at the very last moment and actually bumped into a couple of them before stopping. There were five young men inside.

'Assholes @#$%$*!' yelled Bhaity Da. 'Out! Get out, all of you!'

Bhaity Da was hauling the driver out by the collar when the entirely unexpected happened. The driver headbutted him on the nose and then front-kicked him in the stomach. He went crashing into the road divider.

'@#$%! My nose!' he shouted. It was bleeding. 'Get them!'

Then he noticed that his gang hadn't started beating the crap out of the young men who'd gotten out of the car. He tried to focus through the pain in his nose and saw that all five of them had crew cuts and were wearing similar boots and sweatshirts and jackets. What he couldn't see was the back of their sweatshirts, which happened to read:

Indo-Tibetan Border Police.

TaeKwonDo.

The rest of the goondas couldn't read it either, but their enthusiasm for the goondagiri profession had suddenly died down anyway because the crew-cut young men had all adopted no-nonsense Taekwondo fighting stances. Three of the thugs gulped in a manner worthy of a Tom and Jerry cartoon moment where Tom flashes a very wide appeasing smile at a very pissed-off Spike the bulldog and simultaneously gulps because the rake he had tried to sock Jerry with had missed and poked a sleeping Spike in the butt instead.

In this case, the local goondas were Tom and the ITBP men were Spike the bulldog.

Bhaity Da had probably never learnt any valuable life lessons from Tom and Jerry cartoons, which became evident when, against all the logic of the situation, he shouted, 'Attack!'

The next few seconds made it obvious that his gang hadn't either. You don't mess with a Taekwondo team.

And you certainly don't mess with a Taekwondo team that consists of young armed forces cadets.

Seven local thugs were no match for five trained and fit soldiers. Between them, the seven quickly shared four jabs, eight hooks, six front kicks, eleven roundhouse kicks and two side kicks, distributed over their faces, thighs and midriffs.

Twenty seconds later, Bhaity Da's men were moaning and clutching various parts of their body in pain. One of the ITBP men grabbed his collar and hauled him to his feet, and said, 'We've stopped now. Anything else we can do for you?'

Bhaity Da shook his head without saying a word.

'Good,' said the young policeman, then whirled Bhaity Da around by the collar and shoved him towards the drain. He fell down rolling with a 'Yaaaaaa...!' and landed with a splash in the muddy drain water. Joseph ducked just in time to avoid going down along with him.

The water was very dirty and extremely cold. Bhaity Da, not much of a gang leader now, stood up coughing, various forms of plastic and wild plant life clinging to various parts of his clothing. Derisive laughter sounded all around.

Joseph noticed that the car key had somehow surfaced on Bhaity Da's jacket shoulder. He quickly scooped it up, said thanks, then hot-footed it back up the slope to the car.

'Thank you so much,' he said to the jawans.

'Yes, thank you. You guys are great,' said Aastha.

'No problem,' said a jawan who appeared slightly senior. 'Where are you going?'

'Shillong.'

'Come, you can ride with us till Jorabat.'

'That'd be great,' said Joseph.

As the ITBP men got back into their car, one of them took out a hanky and tossed it towards Bhaity Da, who was climbing out of the drain. 'Here's a towel ha ha ha…'

Another one stuck his arse out towards the thugs and let out a loud, long, carefully selected fart. The Taekwondo soldiers laughed uproariously.

The rest of the journey passed off uneventfully. Once they had crossed the border at Jorabat into Meghalaya territory, the ITBP men waved goodbye and sped off.

Aastha and Joseph paused for breakfast at a restaurant a little beyond Nongpoh, then resumed the three-hour uphill drive.

On the way to Shillong lies the stunningly beautiful Umiam lake, nestled amidst a cluster of beautiful green hills. Just the kind of place poets and composers look for to take up a cottage in and be inspired.

Next to the lake also happens to be the residence of Aastha and Joseph's saviours of the day, the Indo-Tibetan Border Police Academy.

Babita Devi's sister's home in Shillong was in Jenking on top of a small hill with orchid-laden trees.

'Oh my, you've grown so tall and handsome,' said Babita Devi as she welcomed them. 'This your girlfriend, right?'

Joseph looked at Aastha before replying. 'Not exactly.'

'Your mother told me all about her. Said she's a really nice girl. Come in beta, come in. What's your name?'

Half an hour later, Aastha had mercilessly devoured her thirteenth momo from the second batch set out for them. 'Mmm—mmm—she's really nice and her momos are even nicer,' she said.

'Fourteen,' said Joseph, defiantly holding up one and popping it into his mouth. It was too hot. 'Hoo! Ha! Hoo! Hot! Aah!'

In a unique combination, they were having their momos with iromba instead of sauce or red chilly chutney.

Another half hour later, they were sitting on the balcony overlooking a nice little chunk of the locality, sipping herbal tea.

The first brief lull in the conversation gave Joseph the signal to broach the all-important subject. He had no idea how Babita Aunty would react. Four very distinct possibilities existed, three of them very likely, and the fourth, that she would leap up, embrace them and say through tears of joy that this was the very thing she had been expecting and waiting for, about as likely as world peace. The first likely possibility was that she would set the Hound of the Baskervilles on them, except that there were no dogs in the house. The second was that she would reach for the shotgun hanging on the wall and shoot Joseph's precious butt straight to hell, except that luckily there was no shotgun hanging on the wall. Number three was that she would grab his throat with one hand, hoist him high, and then toss him off the balcony onto some rocks below that had been kept sharpened especially for throwing pesky guests on to. This was the most likely. So Joseph swallowed hard, summoned the courage and said:

'Er, Aunty, we need to discuss the real reason we came here.'

'Which is—?'

'Well, it's—um—a few weeks ago, I met Aastha and uh—it so happens that—well—it's complicated—'

Aastha put Joseph out of his misery by bluntly stating, 'I'm looking for somebody to marry my father.'

'Hm?' said Babita Devi, expecting a further punchline. In the three seconds that followed, nobody said anything, then she noticed that both Aastha and Joseph were looking at her funnily, and only then did the full import of Aastha's statement dawn on her.

'Oh,' she said, and her only reaction was to slightly raise her left eyebrow. After another pause, she said, 'I don't think I've ever heard, or will ever hear, anyone ever say that again.'

'Joseph's mother spoke very highly of you, which is why we came to see you.'

'But why do you want your father to marry again, dear? No girl wants a stepmother.'

'I don't want a stepmother. I want a wife for my father.'

'But why?'

'I might be going to the US to study,' said Aastha without batting an eyelid. She had already rehearsed this answer. 'For several years. And when I get married I'll be gone anyway. I don't want Papa to be alone.'

Babita Devi scrutinised Aastha's face. Joseph scrutinised hers for any sign of positive thinking. She took just a teeny-weeny little pause before saying:

'That's really sweet of you, Aastha, but it's really too late for me to be thinking of remarriage.'

'You just want to take care of your grandkids?' said Aastha, taking a calculated risk.

Both Joseph and Aastha detected a very slight mental shudder from Babita Devi.

'Sort of,' she said, not too convincingly.

Aastha threw down her trump card. 'And your loving daughters-in-law?'

It worked. A dark cloud didn't literally cast a shadow over Babita Devi's face, but Aastha could see that mention of the daughters-in-law didn't exactly send her into rapturous sari-clad cartwheels. But Babita Devi put up a brave front. She took a deep breath and said:

'I couldn't do it. What would people say? My sons have been very careful with their political careers and they publicly disapprove of people marrying outside the tribe. If I went ahead and did that, they'd be the laughing-stock of the whole community.'

'But you've already done your duties towards them,' said Aastha. 'They're settled. They've got children of their own. Don't you deserve the rest of your life to yourself?'

'I'm sorry beta. I couldn't be that selfish.'

Joseph sensed that Babita Devi had made her mind up. He said, 'At least meet her father once.'

'What's the use?' she said with a light laugh.

'You don't have to go on dates,' said Aastha. 'Just come to our place for lunch *once.*'

'Ha ha, you're really sweet, but no, my dear.'

'At least have a look at his picture,' said Aastha, opening up her cell gallery and handing it to Babita Devi.

'But what's the use—' said Babita Devi, and suddenly cut herself off mid-sentence when her eyes fell on Aastha's father. 'Oh,' she said after a couple of seconds.

Joseph and Aastha happily noted that the 'Oh' was a mildly-surprised-in-a-good-way 'Oh'.

'When was this taken?' asked Babita Devi. 'Ten years ago?'

'Aunty, we didn't have mobile phones ten years ago,' said Aastha.

'Well... he's not fat and old.'

'No he's not,' said Joseph quickly, eager to lay it on thick. 'He's fitter than me.'

'How come he doesn't look like you?' asked Babita Devi.

'We're thoroughly mixed. Sikkimese Assamese Jharkhandi cocktail.'

Babita Devi stared at the photo a few more seconds more. Good, thought Aastha. Every moment she looks at the photo tilts the scales towards us.

'Please say you'll come to meet him at least once,' said Aastha as sincerely as she could. 'You don't have to talk about marriage or anything. We won't bring it up at all. Just meet like two mature adults and talk about the good old days under Indira Gandhi and how kids these days don't know anything.'

Babita Devi laughed. Excellent, thought Aastha. Defences breaking down.

'Please, Aunty, pleeeeeessssee,' said Joseph.

'Okay, I'll come,' she said finally.

Aastha and Joseph said 'Yes!' and 'Fantastic!' respectively.

'But please don't nurture any expectations from me.'

Joseph thought, I've heard that line before.

'Okay, Aunty,' said Aastha. 'I won't. As far as humanly possible.'

'I somehow think I'm doing something stupid, though.'

'Don't think, Aunty,' said Joseph. 'Just do it.'

Being winter, it would get dark by 5 pm, so they decided to leave as early as possible in order to fit in Aastha's intended sight-seeing of the Don Bosco Church and the Golf Links.

They exchanged warm bye-byes with Babita Devi, who had been made to swear by Aastha to come for lunch the next day.

When the church was in sight, Aastha asked Joseph to park the car while she picked up some medicine from a chemist.

He waited on the church steps and observed Aastha's gait as she came walking from the chemist. Her shoulders very slightly stooped at the corners, and she walked at a pace that indicated haste but also maintained dignity. From the golden gleam, he guessed that the object in her hand was a bar of 5 Star chocolate, and he was right.

'Want some?' she offered.

Joseph took a bite as they entered the church.

'Y'know,' said Joseph. 'There's one thing I can't imagine how I missed asking this whole month that I've known you?'

'What?'

'Your family's Christian?'

'Ma's side is Hindu, Papa is Buddhist, and I prefer Buddha and Jesus.'

'Catholic, Baptist, what?'

'None. I just like the atmosphere of a church. It's peaceful. And I've always loved singing in a choir.'

'I dunno how people manage to sing harmonies. I can barely hold the lead tune. If someone starts doing harmony alongside, I get totally screwed.'

'What about you? Catholic?'

'Well, I've been to a church just once in the last eight years, and that one time was to pee—not in the church itself, of course—and I've been saying that for two years now.'

'Why don't you go?'

'I don't see the point of religion. You can be a good guy without having a god shaking a stick at you. So what's the use of performing one hour of pooja in the morning, then going and looting the public in the day, then coming home and beating your wife at night? I see bad things happening to good people all the time and good things happening to bad people. And He just sits and watches the tamasha. In fact, I don't think He's even around. He probably gave up, packed his bags and moved to another galaxy long ago.'

Green rooms are green because green is the most soothing colour of all, which would perhaps explain the peaceful, easy feeling one gets at the Shillong Golf Links. There's green all around—grass, hills, trees, aliens—er, no, not green aliens—the perfect place for a stroll.

Aastha unwrapped her second chocolate of the day, a Bournville with almonds. Joseph would ordinarily have said something about moderation and the Middle Path, but Aastha was not living an ordinary life.

'We need to find a wife slash girlfriend for you too,' she said, offering Joseph a bite. 'And you're bloody lucky that I know the perfect girl.'

'Who da health?'

'Nadia.'

'Comaneci?'

'No, stupid. She was my best friend in school and college. I'll tell you why she's perfect for you. Number one: she's a singer. Professional. Working her way up the music industry in Mumbai. In fact, I've got the perfect excuse for you to start calling her.'

'What makes you think I'd want to call your friend while you're still around?'

'For a very good reason. My third task for you.'

'Which is—?'

'To get me a date with Arjun Pathania.'

It could have been a misstep into an uneven patch of ground or it could have been plain simple shock that led to Joseph swallowing some chocolate the wrong way. He half-choked and coughed. Aastha thumped him hard on the back a few times and said, 'Are you acting for effect or is this actually happening?'

'Must've been a pothole,' said Joseph, as he drank some water. When he had recovered, he slowly said:

'You want me... to arrange a date for you... with Arjun Pathania?'

'Yup.'

'Why? Why? I mean of all the godforsaken people, why Arjun Pathania?'

'I was in love with him during school and college days. Even before he started acting. When he was still just a supermodel.'

'Of all the people—Arjun Pathania? Are you inspired by *Mili*?'

'Who's Mili?' said Aastha, taking out her cell.

'Never mind. Are you calling your friend right now?'

'Yup. Why delay?'

'This is awkward. Too out of the blue.'

Too late. Aastha turned on the speaker and said, 'Hello-o, darling. What's going on?'

A tired-sounding voice, slightly deeper than Aastha's, said, 'I just peed and did a preg test. Thank God it's negative. I swear I'm not getting drunk around Gaurav anymore.'

Aastha saw that Joseph had broken into a grin. Some first impression he would have had of 'the perfect girl'. For Joseph, those five seconds of conversation had already thrown up three considerably interesting nuggets of information:

1. She had occasional unprotected intercourse.
2. She got drunk sometimes.
3. Usually with some guy named Gaurav.

'Ah-hem!' said Aastha very loudly. 'You're on speaker and Joseph is with me.'

'Shit! You bitch, you did that on purpose,' said Nadia, but she had started laughing the laugh of someone who didn't take herself too seriously. 'Why d'you always call me when I'm in the bathroom, idiot?'

'It's two in the afternoon.'

'I had a late night.'

'Sounds like a laid night. Now say hi to Joseph.'

'I'm a mess!'

'Like he can see you!'

'Hi Joseph.'

'Hello Nadia.'

'Nice to finally talk to you.'

'Wish I could say the same. I mean—it's nice to be introduced, but Aastha never told me about you before.'

'What a possessive bitch ha ha ha. As if I'd steal you from 2500 kilometres away.'

'Shut up, asshole,' said Aastha. 'He's not my boyfriend.'

Joseph was slightly stung, but Aastha's smile was telling him to play along.

'Oh reeeeaaalllllyyyy?' said Nadia. 'So how come half the time you're talking about him?'

'Coincidence.'

'Coincidence my ass and your head. Joseph, she talks about you all the time.'

Joseph said, 'I assure you, they're all lies and baseless allegations.'

Nadia laughed. Aastha showed Joseph a thumbs-up and gave him a pat.

'Um, Nadia,' said Joseph, getting down to business, 'I'm supposed to ask for your help with something'.

'Really? What?'

'Aastha wants me to arrange a date for her with Arjun Pathania.'

'Why am I not surprised?'

'You knew?'

'The day I left for Bombay, she told me to get Arjun Pathania's address if I ever met him. Once she had even married his framed photo with a garland and—'

'Shut up shut up shut up shut up!' interrupted Aastha, and Nadia laughed some more.

'You're not supposed to reveal some secrets,' said Aastha.

'Nor are you supposed to call your pals and ask them to talk with boys on the potty,' said Nadia.

'Okay,' said Joseph, 'are the boys on the potty or are the girls and boys supposed to meet on the potty and talk?'

'Shut up, stupid,' said Aastha, while Nadia let out another laugh.

'Okay, listen,' said Nadia. 'my boyfriend might be knowing someone who knows Pathania. I'll ask and find out.'

'Great. Thanks. Your boyfriend the same guy Gaurav, I hope?'

'Yes, Joseph, the same guy Gaurav. But listen, Pathania or no Pathania, you guys should come over.

I haven't seen Aastha in two years. And I'd sure like to meet you too.'

Aastha winked at Joseph.

'Well, if Arjun Pathania invites her, I'll tag along for sure. To make sure she doesn't molest him—ouch—she kicked me.'

'Well, give her a kick from my side as well, for not coming here to meet me. I gotta flush now, so I'll talk to you guys later, okay.'

'Yeah. Sure. Happy flushing. Nice talking to you.'

'You too. Bye. Bye babe.'

'Bye,' said Aastha, and cut the call. 'Well, stud, you two hit it off *really* well. She's nice, isn't she?'

'She has a boyfriend.'

'So what? He's an asshole. Sooner or later she'll see sense and dump him.'

'That's a funny thing about real life. All the great girls go to the assholes of the world and the good guys wind up with the queen bitches.'

'That usually happens with first loves. They get wiser after that.'

'By the way, what's the fourth task?'

'Later, when the time is right... Last piece?'

Joseph took the last piece of chocolate. There wasn't anywhere to throw the wrapper, so Aastha stuffed it into the butt pocket of Joseph's jeans.

Suddenly, Joseph felt his butt being pinched.

'Oi!' he exclaimed. Aastha was devilishly giggling. 'What're you doin'?' he said. 'There's family public around.'

Aastha said, 'I've always wanted to do that. Sexually abuse a nice guy. Preferably in public.' Then she slapped him on the butt.

'Oi! Pervert,' said Joseph, and scampered a few steps away, his ass in his hands. Aastha was still laughing.

Night had settled by the time they reached Jorabat on the way back.

'What d'you think?' said Joseph. 'Your dad's gonna be keen to marry?'

Chapter 16

Role Reversal

'No,' said Mr Mishra after dinner that night. 'Are you crazy? No way. How could you even think—no, no and no.'

'It's not for your sake, Papa. I'm doing it out of pure selfish motives. I want to know you'll have something to look forward to, someone to come home to. I don't want to leave you behind alone.'

'Don't ever say such things, and that's not the point.'

'Papa, don't make me blackmail you emotionally. I don't want you to become one of those lonely cranky old men who don't have anything to keep them occupied and end up doing nothing but lamenting, "This country is going to the dogs".'

'It *is*!'

'See? First symptoms already.'

'That's not the point.'

'You're right. That's not the point. Look, Papa, all I'm saying is meet her once. That's all. Just meet her. You don't have to start actively dating and going to movies and coffee shops and shady parks. Just one lunch. You might see a one per cent glimmer of something for the future, not for right now. She's not going anywhere and neither are you.'

'How will I adjust, beta? I've lived all my life just with you.'

'Exactly, Papa.'

Father and daughter exchanged silent looks. Mr Mishra sighed and Aastha jumped at the chance. She opened the photos of Babita Devi she'd taken on her cell and said, 'Just one lunch,' then handed it to her father.

'What's the use when—oh.'

Mr Mishra's reaction on seeing Babita Devi's picture was the same as hers on seeing him. Cut off mid-sentence. Aastha smiled.

'She's not very old,' said Mr Mishra.

'She's got grandkids.'

'Grandkids!'

'Doesn't look like it, right?'

'Yes, no. Looks like her children would be in their teens.'

'Great. I'm glad you like her looks, to start with. I'm sure you'll be able to charm the socks off her.'

Mr Mishra frowned at the odd expression, then said, 'When d'you plan to invite her?'

'I already have. Tomorrow.'
'Tomorrow!?!'
'Yup. Why delay?'

Local historians will have noted that Babita Devi arrived for lunch the next day at 11.26 am, in a car driven by a tough-looking nut named Babu, who looked like you would need his written permission to crack a joke, even one totally unrelated to himself, his family or his race. He was the driver-cum-bodyguard Joseph's mother had spoken of. He declined to come into the house, possibly preferring the outdoors in the hope that some poor soul passing by would provoke him and he could kill some time by bashing them up.

The concept of a prospective groom's family going to a girl's house to have a look at the girl is something that has puzzled innumerable noted scientists over the millenia. If the boy has been dragged there by his parents, he spends his time sulking and looking at the table in front of him. If he's the sort who's never been able to get a girl in his life and is depending on his folks to do that too for him, he spends his time ogling the girl every chance he gets. The girl comes in with tea, one parent says their daughter is a wonderful cook, the other parent says she can sing very well, and insists that the poor girl do so, and if the groom's family likes the tea and snacks and the girl's singing and her looks, then they say okay, let's get the poor saps married. So the boy thinks he's got it made until the day after the wedding when this shy, simple girl he thought he was getting married to turns out to be a tigress of the first order. And if he's really unlucky, his parents, before the proposal, wouldn't have gotten a private detective to thoroughly investigate the girl's antecedents, and the new wife turns out to be the psycho husband-killer who did away with seven husbands, none of whose bodies was ever found.

Most of the abovementioned has absolutely nothing to do with the events that transpired at lunch that day, except that there were two reversals. One: instead of the groom's side going to the bride's, the bride came to the groom's home. Two: the children became the parents and the parents became the children.

It all started with the mention of tea. Aastha said, 'Papa, let's have your special tea now, shall we?'

'Okay,' said Mr Mishra, and stood up.

Until then, things had gone by with as little awkwardness as possible in such a situation. Both Mr Mishra and Babita Devi could feel two pairs of eyes, Aastha's and Joseph's, microscopically focused on every interaction between the two of them. The two seniors were trying to strike a delicate balance between not being so friendly that Aastha would jump the gun and not being so cold as to be termed rude.

As Mr Mishra took his first step towards the kitchen, Aastha said to Babita Devi, 'Papa makes the best ginger tea in the world. Today he's also prepared some malpuwa for you.'

'That's—that's nice,' replied the prospective stepmother.

'Not to mention the lovely chicken he's made for lunch,' said Aastha.

'Tone down the trumpet, will you?' said Mr Mishra, already feeling slightly embarrassed.

A few minutes later, he emerged from the kitchen with a tray laden with tea and malpuwas. Of course, since he wasn't a shy young eligible girl, there was no aunty by his side prodding him on with a wide smile.

Click! Aastha captured the moment on her cell. Mr Mishra's face was frozen in one of those priceless 'Eh? What happened?' expressions.

'Looking cute, Papa,' said Aastha casually. Mr Mishra chose to be stoic and ignored the remark.

Babita Devi took a sip of the tea and said, 'Ah, this is really very nice.' And for the first time since being introduced, she had relaxed and made a totally unaffected comment.

'Thanks,' said Mr Mishra, smiling back.

'Try the malpuwa too,' offered Aastha.

Babita Devi had a malpuwa and then said, 'Hm, even this is very nice. You're a good cook. I'm surprised your daughter isn't fat.'

'Heh. Thanks,' said Mr Mishra, smiling like a newly manufactured teenager who has just been complimented by a girl for the first time.

Seeing her father still a little awkward, Aastha piled it on a bit more. 'That's because Papa's very health-conscious. He's quite slim for a man his age.'

'Thank you very much beta. Now take your tea,' said Mr Mishra, but the subtext in his tone was, 'Will you please shut up.'

'Joseph, you too,' he added.

'Er, yes, Uncle,' said Joseph, watching the proceedings as neutrally as possible.

Aastha took a cup of tea and some malpuwas for Babu the tough guy as well. She said to him, 'Please let us know if you need anything else.'

'Hmg,' said Babu.

Back inside, when the tea was done, Aastha said, 'Y'know Aunty, Papa's a wonderful singer too.'

Mr Mishra shot at Aastha a look that pleaded, 'What're you doing!' but it fell on deaf ears and ignoring eyes.

Aastha continued. 'He used to win all his college singing competitions. And obviously, he's an All-India Radio registered singer.'

'Mummyji,' said Mr Mishra, embarassed to the point where he was sure people would see him blushing if they looked carefully, 'please stop blowing my trumpet.'

'Papa, sing us a song, please. Even Joseph hasn't heard you sing.'

'Oh come on. I have hardly any practice.'

'You were practising last night with the harmonium.'

If looks could kick...

'Joseph, get the guitar,' ordered Aastha. 'In fact, Aunty, why don't the two of you sing a duet?'

Both the prospective bride and groom protested. Aastha cut them off and said, 'Oh please please... Sing a golden oldie. *Gaate Rahe Mera Dil* or *Ehsan Tera Hoga Mujhpar* or *Dekha Ek Khwab*.'

'I don't remember the lyrics,' said Mr Mishra.

'Papa, stop making silly excuses. These are some of the songs you never forget. And anyway, I know you have the lyrics and chords written in your diary.'

Mr Mishra wondered for a few seconds what he had done to deserve this, then he looked at his daughter's earnestness—the enthusiasm in her smile—and he melted and crossed over to the other side, going from 'Oh god no' to 'Oh what the hell.'

'Okay,' he said, smiling now. 'Get the diary.'

The singing turned out to be the highlight of the day. Some people are not at all shy and are ever ready to burst into song at picnics and parties and reality shows, their only minor flaws being a wonderful inability to hit even a single note correctly and a total lack of awareness of this tiny hindrance. Such people ought to be told to save it for the bathroom, preferably a soundproof one so that fellow inmates and neighbours can live life in peace, but unfortunately they're usually the ones who inflict on innocent bystanders their misguided attempts at melody. People who can actually sing, on the other hand, rarely make a show of it. Those among them who are also shy need a lot of prodding and encouragement, but once they get off the blocks, the notes just flow.

Babita Devi turned out to belong to the latter category. Aastha had to threaten to literally fall at her feet before she finally started singing, but when she did, there was no doubt that singing could be added to cooking in her list of talents.

'Wonderful,' said Aastha as they all clapped at the end. 'Well then, Joseph, come into the kitchen and help me arrange the food. I think we should leave the boy and the girl alone together for a little while—let them get to know each other.'

Mr Mishra grabbed Aastha's ear and twisted it.

'Ow ow ow, okay, okay, sorry Papa. But you're almost blushing—ow! Ouch, okay, I won't say anything. Joseph, let's go.'

Off the two went into the kitchen. In the hall, Babita Devi looked around at the paintings and pictures which, naturally, she was seeing for the first time, and Mr Mishra looked around and intently studied the sofa and the tables which he had been seeing every day for the last eighteen years of his life. Then he suddenly realised that the kitchen seemed to be very quiet.

'You two can stop eavesdropping,' he said.

'Sorry, Papa,' said Aastha sheepishly. Both of them had been standing near the kitchen door.

When Mr Mishra could actually hear the clatter of dishes, he relaxed a bit and said, 'You sing very well.'

'Quite rusty though,' said Babita Devi, breaking into a smile.

'Doesn't seem so at all. And you don't even look like you have grandchildren.'

'I got married when I was sixteen.'

'Early start, eh?'

In the kitchen, Aastha said to Joseph, 'Well, they're talking now.'

'Listen, I've had this idea for quite some time. I want to record some songs with you.'

'Eh? Smack out of the blue. Why?'

'What d'you mean why? Because you're a great singer and I'm a not-too-bad composer. That's obvious.'

Aastha was silent for a few moments before answering. 'Let's ask Babita Aunty to record some songs with Papa. That way, they'll get to spend time together.'

'That's a very good idea.'

'And while we're at it, let's also get them stuck somewhere on a deserted highway on a rainy night near an abandoned house in a jungle with some firewood and only one blanket inside.'

'This might have worked in the '80s.'

'You're right. And there'd be a kabab mein haddi anyway,' said Aastha, discreetly pointing at Babu the bodyguard, whom they could see through the window.

'But what about us? You singing?'

Aastha again paused before saying, 'Joseph, I think it'd be better if you didn't have any memories of me to cling to. It'll be harder for you to move on.'

'Do I look like I want to move on?' said Joseph, three ladles in one hand and a pressure cooker in the other.

'Shut up and take them to the dining table.'

A few minutes later, Joseph served Babu his lunch. To his consternation, he noticed in the small of Babu's back a lump that could only be a gun.

'Eat away,' said Joseph, trying to be cheerful.

'Hmg,' said Babu.

Back in the kitchen, Joseph whispered to Aastha, 'He's packing heat.'

'My God. What for? Who'd want to do anything to a nice lady like her?... D'you think her sons would order him to shoot us if they found out what we're trying to do?'

'Shall I ask him?... But he'd probably just say 'Hmg'. Which language is that anyway?'

'Gruffian?'

An hour later it was time to say goodbye.

'Well, do think about Joseph's idea,' said Mr Mishra to Babita Devi as she got into the car. 'I think a fine voice like yours should be recorded.'

'Absolutely,' said Aastha.

'Let's see,' said Babita Devi.

Father, daughter and one-sided lover waved goodbye to prospective stepmother as the car drove away.

'So, Papa, did you like her?'

'You little badtameez,' said Mr Mishra, grabbing her ear.

'Ow! But you're smiling! That means you liked her—youch! Ow! Okay, sorry. But don't worry—I'll give you her number.'

'I have it,' said Mr Mishra suavely, as though he was performing in a gentlemen's suiting ad.

'Ohhhhhh you already do. How very smart. My Papa the playboy—ow! Aaaaaaa...'

CHAPTER 17

Debuting In a New Field of Enterprise

THE ABOVEMENTIONED NEW FIELD OF ENTERPRISE happened to be kidnapping, or rather, mothernapping. We'll get to that, but first, a brief history of the intervening days:

Without the need for any convincing by Joseph, Aastha changed her mind about recording songs, and they began in right earnest. Over the next three weeks, Joseph polished the music of three songs he had composed and arranged, and they recorded Aastha's vocals at the Srimanta Sankardev Kalakhetra studio.

A lot of people sound really good when they sing on stage or around friends and family, but the studio microphone really separates the wheat from the chaff. Just like many people suddenly freeze and become awkward in front of a video camera, many singers get nervous when they stand in front of a microphone and the metronome starts ticking. None of this happened to Aastha. Furthermore, most proper singers can hit the right notes, but few have that extra ability to add the right depth and emotion to go along with the notes. Aastha was one of those gifted singers who poured the exact nuances and feelings into every word.

On the other hand, Joseph's feeling of being thoroughly doomed worsened with every vocal recording session as he fell more and more in love with the singing angel that Aastha was. Several times, he tried to convince himself that the revelations she had made that night at IIT were all part of one of his ghastly nightmares, but it was impossible. Every occasion that Aastha pigged out on food, especially chocolate, served as a reminder that this was a girl who knew she didn't have much time left and was trying to make the most of her last few days or years.

Unknown to Aastha, her father had started calling Babita Devi, but not before several pacing-up-and-down deliberations and picking up the phone and putting it down again.

A few weeks after that first phone call, Babita Devi decided to record Joseph's song after all.

'Forget it, Ma,' said Hansen, Babita Devi's elder son, without looking away from the TV, which was showing local news. 'Who are these people? Are they going to pay you or something?'

'I'm not doing it for money. I just want to sing. It's been a long time.'

Hansen's children had started yelling in the corridor. Citizens unlucky enough to know them would swear they made Dennis the Menace and Calvin look like sweet little inanimate teddy bears.

'Oi! Keep it down!' Hansen shouted. Then he said to his mother, still not looking at her, 'So we'll book a studio here and you can sing. Why d'you have to go all the way there?'

Babita Devi couldn't find an appropriate answer. One of kids screamed again, and Hansen shouted, 'If you don't shut up, you're gonna get super-dhulai!'

A few seconds of peace and quiet followed, during which Babita Devi said, 'You're behaving as though *you're* my father.'

'Don't be silly, Ma,' said Hansen, eyes still glued to a potential political opponent on TV. 'Why do you have to go around with people we don't know? Stay with us and play with your grandkids.'

'They hate me.'

'That's because you're always telling them to bathe daily and do their homework and not eat chips.'

There really isn't much one can say in reply to such a statement. Babita Devi was fishing for words when a loud crash sounded from one of the rooms.

'That does it!' said Hansen, and stormed off to deal with the disturbance.

'I hate them too,' murmured Babita Devi.

Two days later, Joseph opened the door to a very excited Aastha.

'Yes! Yes! Yes! She said yes!' she said.

'You finally proposed to your secret girlfriend?'

'No, to my dad's wife-to-be. She told Papa yesterday that she's had enough of her selfish kids and shaitan ke aulad grandkids.'

'Eh? Just like that?'

'Oh, no, not just like that. Papa turned out to be an A-grade player. These last few weeks he's been secretly calling her. And now she's ready to take a chance on him.'

'Her sons have agreed?'

'Ha ha. She wants to elope.'

'At her age?'

'She wants to show them the finger, I suppose.'

'So how are we gonna do it? Chloroform hanky on the bodyguard's nose?'

So they schemed. In a couple of weeks, Babita Devi would feign some illness, not too serious, for which she would need to come to a hospital in Guwahati. On her way back, she would feed Babu the bodyguard some coconut larus laced with a herb that was a powerful cure for constipation. Babu would need to take a walk in a rose garden somewhere, and in that time, Babita Devi would let herself be abducted.

On the appointed day, the three would-be kidnappers, Aastha, Utpal and Joseph, waited in their car near a cluster of shops in Sonapur, a tiny town on the outskirts of Guwahati which has several resorts and dhabas.

Aastha stepped out to buy a couple of medicines from a pharmacy. As she paid, her cell beeped. It was a message from Babita Devi: Passing through Sonapur.

Aastha rushed back into the car. 'She's coming.'

'No, she's gone!' said Joseph. 'Her car just passed. Get in, quick!'

The message had probably been delivered late because Babita Devi had been passing through a no-network area. Aastha dived into the car and Joseph hit the accelerator.

Babu was a fast driver, and Joseph, who preferred to be on the safer side of the laws of physics, had to take corners at speeds he had never attempted in his life before.

'Try not to kill us,' said Utpal, trying to sound as casual as possible, whereas his heart was actually playing a double bass drum roll.

From her car, Babita Devi could make out that Joseph was having a hard time keeping up with Babu's almost-maniacal driving.

'Take it, easy, Babu. I'm getting a little nervous.'

Babu didn't reply, but he eased up on the speed a bit, and Joseph managed to get within range.

A few minutes later, Babu said, 'That car's been following us?'

Babita Devi looked back and saw that Joseph was too close for comfort. She said, 'Everyone's going the same way.'

'I've given him chances to overtake but he hasn't.'

'Oh, don't be paranoid, Babu.'

But Babu wasn't too sanguine. It was his job to be paranoid.

Babita Devi sent a message to Aastha, telling her to keep a safe distance or Babu would recognise them.

'Fall back a bit,' said Aastha.

Joseph let a comfortable distance grow between the cars.

When Babu looked in his rearview mirror a minute later, the other car was out of sight. 'Maybe they realised that *we* realised they were following us.'

'You're being unnecessarily paranoid,' said Babita Devi. 'Here, have a laru.'

'No thanks, Ma. I don't like coconut larus.'

'Shut up. What kind of person doesn't like coconut larus? Have at least one. I made them myself.'

Reluctantly, Babu took a laru and popped it into his mouth.

At last, thought Babita Devi. That one laru would be enough to send anyone rushing for the nearest commode within minutes.

'Hm, it's actually quite good,' said Babu. 'Can I have another?'

'Oops. I just had the last one,' said Babita Devi, and quickly hid the remaining larus in her bag. She didn't want Babu to excrete his bowels altogether.

As expected, within a few minutes, Babu felt the first gurgling in his stomach. A gigantic bubble seemed to form in his intestines.

'Er, Ma, can we make a quick stop at a dhaba?'

'Of course.'

Babu speeded up to get to the next dhaba or restaurant as quickly as possible. He didn't have to go too far. There was one beside a petrol pump, and the car tyres screeched as he parked with action-film flair.

'I'll be right back,' said Babu, making a run for it.

Within a minute, Joseph had also pulled over into the parking area, a few cars away from Babita Devi's.

'Quick, get my bag out,' she said as she stepped out.

Joseph got into the back seat and tried to lift the huge airbag out of the dicky, but it was too big, and got stuck between the seat and the hatch. Joseph grunted and pulled, but it was firmly wedged.

'Oh no, Babu's out,' said Babita Devi. 'Get down, quick. Hide.'

Joseph got onto the floor of the car behind the driver's seat. Displaying some quick thinking, Babita Devi threw her shawl over him.

'Crap,' said Aastha in her car, making sure to stay out of Babu's line of sight.

'Shit shit shitty shittety shit shit,' said Utpal.

Babu smiled a queer smile and said to Babita Devi, 'False alarm.' Then he noticed the stuck bag and took a step towards the back door. 'You wanted something from the bag?'

'No, never mind. I got it. Let's go,' said Babita Devi, stepping in front of Babu so he wouldn't see Joseph crouching behind.

'Okay,' said Babu. They both got into the car.

As Babu reversed and zoomed off, Aastha said, 'Holy quackerooney.'

'We're screwed,' said Utpal.

Aastha hurriedly got into the driver's seat and started the car. It was time for really hot pursuit.

'Damn,' said Utpal. 'What do we do now? My mother didn't raise me to kidnap other people's mothers.'

Crouched on all fours, Joseph was beginning to feel pins and needles at various points of his body. He had to resist a strong urge to cough on a couple of occasions. Making as little movement as possible, he extracted his cell phone from his pocket and sent Aastha a message: Send me her number.

'Utpal,' said Aastha, handing him her phone, 'send Joseph Babita Devi's number'.

After about a minute, the number arrived. Then Joseph messaged Babita Devi: Hi Aunty. Joseph here. I don't think this was a very good idea.

Babita Devi looked slightly startled to see the message, coming as it did from someone who was literally right at her feet. She replied: I'm thinking.

The message reached Joseph's cell and it beeped. Teet-teet. Teet-teet. Oh crap, thought Joseph, and mentally slapped himself. He quickly switched his cell to silent mode.

Babu had heard the beeping, but assumed it to **be** Babita Devi's cell.

Babita Devi sent Joseph another message: Maybe you should keep your mobile on silent.

Joseph wrote back: I just did.

The absurdity of messaging someone literally just a foot away from oneself wasn't lost on Joseph.

So far, Babita Devi had displayed an ability to think fast on her feet on a couple of occasions. She decided to try an old trick once again.

'Oh, how silly of me. There're some more larus left, Babu. Have another.'

'I think I'll pass, Ma. Stomach might react.'

'Nonsense. I thought you said they were nice,' she said, trying to sound injured. 'Here, have one more.'

Babu took the laru and put it in his mouth. If even this one doesn't work, thought Babita Devi, Babu needs to put himself up as a specimen for anatomical research.

But her concerns proved to be unfounded this time. The herb, probably offended at Babu's denial of its potency, attacked his bowels once again with renewed vigour.

Blop-blub-blurp. Babu distinctly heard these gurgling sounds coming from his stomach, and then he distinctly felt pressure of considerably high Toricelli in his bowels. There was no way to hold it back.

'Ma, I think I'm going to have to stop in the bushes.'

'Oh, okay,' said Babita Devi. 'I think coconut doesn't agree with you.'

Babu stopped the car near an appreciably dense thicket beside the road.

'Leave the key,' said Babita Devi.

Babu took a bottle of water and ran into the bushes. When he was out of sight, Babita Devi pulled the shawl off Joseph.

'Let's go, hurry. Drive.'

Joseph scrambled out and immediately felt a thousand needles and pins. 'Ouch ouch ow.'

He got into the driver's seat and started the car. As he made a U-turn, Babu, who had heard the sounds and immediately gotten suspicious, came running from behind the bushes, zipping up his pants.

'Oi! Oi! Dammit!' he exclaimed and ran back to the bushes to get his gun, which he had set aside before starting to answer nature's second call.

Gun in hand, Babu ran out on to the road, but Joseph had already driven off and disappeared behind a big bamboo grove at a bend. Babu let forth a volley of curses.

As luck would have it, another car slowed down and came to a stop just a little distance from him. The driver, a bespectacled young professional-looking man named Ratan, alighted and headed for the very same bushes which had hosted Babu not too long ago.

Babu saw his chance. He ran to the car and got in, but the ignition was sans the key.

'Oi! You!' he yelled at Ratan. 'Get back in here!'

Ratan looked back. Was someone yelling at him?

'You!' shouted Babu. 'The pissing guy! Come here at once!'

'What the hell,' muttered Ratan and arrested his flow midway. Who was this lunatic in his car?

He walked back and said to Babu, 'Who the hell are you and what—don't kill me!' The change in tone was brought about by the gun Babu had shoved in his face.

'Shut up and get in.'

'Please don't kill me.'

'I won't if you start driving. Fast!'

Ratan got in and started the car.

'U-turn! Quick!'

'But I'm going that way.'

Babu couldn't believe that anyone could raise such stupid objections even in the face of a gun. He pulled off Ratan's specs with his gun-wielding hand, and gave him a slap with his other. Thwack! Yow! Then he replaced the specs.

'Want some more?'

'Don't shoot me, please.'

'Shut up and turn!'

Ratan made a quick turn. It was now Babu's turn to chase. 'Faster, faster.'

Ratan put on his seat belt. Babu couldn't believe that anyone could bother about *seat belts* when there was a *gun* pointed at their head.

Less than two kilometres away, Joseph and Babita Devi had rejoined the other mothernappers. Joseph hurriedly opened the hatch and carried Babita Devi's huge bag into Aastha's car. Then, with a rather silly flourish, he tossed Babu's keys high behind him into the air. They landed with a clink right in the middle of the road in plain sight.

'What're you doing?' said Aastha.

'Oh, sorry.'

'Bring the keys,' said Babita Devi. 'We'll arrange to give them back later.'

Joseph retrieved the keys, pressed the lock button and then rushed back into Aastha's car.

'Welcome aboard,' said Aastha to Babita Devi as she sped off.

A couple of minutes later, Babu and Ratan chanced upon the deserted car. Babu took a quick look. The doors were locked and the key wasn't inside.

'Drive, drive! Fast!'

Meanwhile, in the other car, Babita Devi said, 'I haven't eloped in a very lonnnng time. This is fun.'

Joseph wasn't sure he shared that sentiment, there being the very real possibility that a very pissed-off bodyguard would shoot his arse to hell and give him unnecessary new body orifices. Utpal was doubly concerned. He was not only worried about getting shot, but was also praying that his beliefs about women being naturally bad drivers would be proven wrong and Aastha would get them home and dry with each of their 206 bones intact.

Babita Devi looked back. No car in sight yet.

'Poor Babu,' she said, and dialled his number on her cell.

Babu saw her number on his cell and was sure it was the kidnappers calling.

'Hello!' he said rudely.

'Babu, it's me. I'm all right.'

'Ma, what's going on? Are you okay?'

'I'm quite okay. Listen, I'm running away to get married.'

'What?' Babu was sure he had heard wrong.

'I'm running away to get married.'

'What!' Not bothering to make sense of what he thought he had just heard, Babu said, 'Listen Ma, keep calm, don't worry. I'm right behind you. I'll rescue you and kill those bastards.'

'Oh my God, no. You don't understand. You don't have to rescue me. I'm running away of my own free will. Hansen would never have let me go, so I decided to do it this way.'

'Eh? But—why're you running away?'

'I told you—to get married.'

'Married?' The concept seemed highly alien to Babu. 'To whom?'

'Never mind to whom. He's a good man and I think we'll be happy together.'

'... Ma—how can you do this? Look, I'm sorry—I can't let you go just like that. I'll have to take you to Hansen. He'll decide.'

'Babu, *I'm* his mother, not the other way round. So just turn back and go home.'

'Sorry, Ma. I have to do my duty,' said Babu, and cut the call. 'Drive faster!' he said to a petrified Ratan.

'Aargh!' exclaimed Babita Devi. 'What a thick skull. Poor fellow.'

A few minutes later, they crossed the Jorabat intersection. A barricaded police checkpost was on the road ahead.

'Here's our chance,' said Aastha as she slowed down to speak to a potbellied havaldar.

'Excuse me, Dada. There's a car behind us, and we're not sure, but I think there's a man with a gun inside.'

'What car is it?'

'It's a black Zen,' said Babita Devi.

'We'll take care of it,' said the policeman, then gave his men orders. 'Oi, get your guns ready. There's a car coming. Might be armed.'

'Give me Babu's keys,' said Babita Devi to Joseph. Then she handed the keys to the havaldar and said, 'We found these on the road.'

The havaldar took the keys and scratched his head. A constable scratched his arse. Another constable scratched his family jewels.

As Aastha's kidnapping gang drove off, they saw three policemen take position, with guns ready.

In less than two minutes, Ratan and Babu had also reached Jorabat. As they crossed the intersection, they saw two policemen aiming their rifles at their car and a havaldar signalling them to stop.

'They've got guns,' said Ratan, in a state of panic by now.

'Just put your head down and crash through. Don't stop,' said Babu with authority.

'They'll shoot us if we don't.'

'And I'll shoot you if you do.'

The havaldar was now shouting threats and waving at them to stop. Ratan accelerated. He was just about twenty or thirty metres from the barricade when—screech!—he hit the brakes with full force.

Babu's head slammed into the windshield with a loud bonk! Then it slowly slid down with a squeaky sound onto the dashboard. He was out cold.

Ratan was almost hyperventilating, but it was also out of relief that his oppressor was now knocked out. He looked up in the direction of his home and said, 'Thank you Ma, for always insisting that I wear a seat belt.'

Chapter 18

Hyperactive Imagination

To cut a long story short, Babu had to spend a couple of days in jail before Hansen managed to pull several strings and get him out. Ratan was too thankful to have escaped without a hole in his head to pursue any proceedings against Babu, the mere sight of whom would have given him the jitters anyway.

The next day, Mr Mishra and Babita Devi got married at the registrar's office in Guwahati with just closest friends and family in attendance. Dinner that night was a joint preparation by the newlyweds. Joseph and Utpal ate the most they had in a year.

Joseph imagined what the scene would be like if Hansen had gone to the police.

Officer-in-Charge: What's the problem?
Hansen: My mother eloped.
OC: You mean your daughter.
Hansen: No. My mother.

OC: You mean your mother?
Hansen: Yes. My mother. Eloped.
OC: Hahahahahahahaha... (falls off chair and dies laughing).

Three days later, daughter, father, new stepmother and non-boyfriend landed at the domestic airport in Mumbai. After exchanging goodbyes and emotional hugs, the first two headed for another terminal to catch a flight to Goa, while the latter two made for the exit.

'Now we meet *your* future wife,' said Aastha.

'Oh really?'

Nadia was waiting for them at the arrivals gate. The two girls jumped and waved at each other, then hugged heartily when they were within range. Joseph took a good look at Nadia. She had shoulder-length hair, wore a nose ring and had lined her large eyes thickly. She was only a little less slim than Aastha, and her top and short skirt flattered her figure well.

After the hugs were done with, Nadia turned to Joseph.

'Hi Joseph.'

'Hi Nadia,' said Joseph, and shook hands.

'Oh you already like each other,' said Aastha. 'A match made in heaven—ow!' Both of them had smacked her on one shoulder each.

Later that evening, Joseph got a demonstration of why Aastha thought Nadia would be the perfect match for him—she was an equally fabulous singer, and a keyboard player to boot. The girls sang a few songs, alternating between lead and harmony, while Joseph played guitar on the songs that he knew too.

'Better than me, isn't she?' said Aastha when they had a moment alone.

'She's amazing, but I wouldn't say better than you.'

'Her bass notes are more solid, and she's better than me at classical stuff.'

'Well, she's a professional. I'm sure you'll be just as good if you practise.'

'She's got great legs, eh?'

'I'm sure yours are just as good—if you—'

'If I what, eh?'

'Um, if you'll let me make an objective evaluation.'

Aastha rapped Joseph on the head and said, 'Be faithful to her. Don't already start thinking about other girls' legs.'

'What other girls? I was just talking about your legs, not hers. And she's got a bloody boyfriend.'

'I'm telling you again: she'll see the light one day, kick him between the legs and leave him.'

Right on cue, the hall door opened and Nadia's boyfriend Gaurav stepped in. Joseph had visualised a cliched good-looking, well-dressed, tall, muscular boyfriend, but Gaurav fit only the 'tall' specification. He was unshaven, unkempt and scrawny—not at all the kind of bloke one would expect an enormously talented, pretty girl like Nadia to fall for. But then again, as Joseph and Aastha had previously discussed, the good girls always seem to go to the assholes of the world.

'Hi, Aastha!' said Gaurav very loudly. 'Still looking as smoking hot as ever!'

Joseph thought, *I'll* make you sit on something smoking hot.

'Gaurav,' said Gaurav, extending a hand.

'Joseph,' said Joseph, shaking it.

The next half-hour of conversation did nothing to improve Joseph's impression of Gaurav as a stick-in-the-mud who peddled dishevelment and cynicism as world-weary sophistication. What a girl like Nadia saw in him was beyond Joseph. Maybe that kind of 'maturity' was attractive to girls for the first few months or so.

Aastha and Nadia had gone out to get some food and groceries. The only shred of redemption Joseph found in Gaurav's company was that Gaurav knew someone who was working on an ad which feaured Arjun Pathania, and coincidentally, that chap happened to be Assamese as well.

'He's coming now,' said Gaurav.

'Oh good. What's his name?'

'I keep forgetting. Rajkamal something.'

Two minutes later the doorbell rang. And who should walk through the door but—

Tonmoy!

Joseph froze. Here was the s-o-b and s-in-the-g who had stabbed him in the back and stolen his girlfriend!

'Joseph?' said Tonmoy, momentarily stunned.

'It's you? You backstabbing asshole.'

'You know Rajkamal?' said Gaurav to Joseph.

'My name is Tonmoy,' said the owner of the name stiffly.

'Shit. Sorry. Don't know why I always mix it up. Always happens with similar names.'

'Tonmoy sounds *nothing* like Rajkamal.'

'Don't try to change the subject,' said Joseph. Then he said to Gaurav, 'I hope you haven't given this guy the numbers of your girlfriends or sisters or mothers. No one's safe from him.'

'Don't overreact,' said Tonmoy.

' "Don't overreact?" "Don't overreact"?'! You have the nerve to tell me not to overreact! You girlfriend-stealing rotten bastard.'

Under normal circumstances, Joseph would have blown his fuse, charged and tackled Tonmoy. Then straddling him, he would have put on a pair of boxing gloves that would have magically materialised out of nowhere and rained punches on him, then taken a guitar and broken it on his head, then borrowed some shock-therapy equipment from the nearest mental hospital and given him 220-volt electric shocks, taken a break for tea, and then possibly repeated the procedure again.

But then Tonmoy said: 'She left me.'

'Eh?'

'She dumped me. Uma.'

Now this was a totally unexpected bit of news. Joseph felt a pin puncture his balloon of anger. '… Oh. Congratulations… Now why would she do that?'

'She's screwing her way up the ladder. Doing her boss now.'

Joseph took a good look at Tonmoy's face. It looked so very wounded that he couldn't help a snort. Then he chuckled. Then the chuckle turned into laughter.

'I thought she loved me,' said Tonmoy.

If Tonmoy had expected that statement to get him some sympathy, he was totally off the mark. Joseph's laughter only intensified. He spent about half a minute laughing.

When the laughter had subsided, he said, 'Y'know what, I thought I'd kill you when I met you, but I really don't care now. I wasn't really angry. She doesn't matter one tiny rat's ass anymore.'

'She was one hell of a bitch.'

Joseph thought about it. Time had given him some objectivity. 'Not really. At least not in my view. She did the right thing by leaving me, or maybe I'd never have grown up. If it was my sister or someone in her place, I too would probably have told her to dump a good-for-nothing boyfriend.'

Tonmoy wondered for a second whether Joseph had been spending too much time near a Jesus ashram, then he declared simply, 'She was one hell of a bitch... I was just a few months with her. How did you get through five years? You should line up for a Republic Day bravery medal. I'm telling you, whoever marries her is gonna jump in front of a local train or admit himself into an asylum within a year.'

'If she doesn't stab him with scissors first.'

'Good God! She tried to do that to you too?'

'Yup. I've still got a small mark on my arm.'

'I've got it in my back. Psycho bitch.'

'Did she try to squeeze your eyes in?'

'No, but she kicked me almost in the family jewels when I was lying down.'

'She hit me on the head with a half-litre bottle of lotion.'

'She threw a DVD player at my head. Luckily, I ducked.'

'She emptied a ladleful of chicken gravy on me in a restaurant.'

'Shit! You too! In my case it was corn soup.'

Joseph laughed. He was actually bonding with a bloke whom he would instead have been strangling a minute ago. They shared a common history of having been through hell.

'Psycho bitch,' said Tonmoy.

A few minutes later, they were all chomping down on frankies and sandwiches brought by the girls.

'Remember what you said at Santonu's birthday treat at U-Turn?' said Aastha to Nadia.

'Yeah. Funny how the guys always seem to order momos and the girls order rolls.'

No one got the significance of the remark for a second. Then the two girls looked very pointedly at Joseph, who had one end of a long frankie in his mouth, ready to bite. They started laughing.

'Oh,' said Joseph, his bulb lighting up.

'But she was always the exception,' said Nadia of Aastha, 'going for momos most of the time. Is that where your preferences lie, eh?'

'Darling,' said Aastha, 'if that were the case, I would have attacked *your* momos long ago.'

'You girls are vulgar,' said Joseph as the girls cackled. He stuck the frankie in his mouth to take another bite and their laughter became even more ribald.

'How juvenile,' said Joseph. 'Someone give me a sandwich.'

The clock struck one when they finally decided to call it a night. Nadia brought a mattress into the hall and shot Aastha a questioning glance. Aastha's answer was:

'Joseph, you sleep on the couch. I'll take the mattress.'

Aastha fell asleep almost immediately, whereas Joseph contemplated his situation for a bit. Here he was in the same room with the girl he loved more than he had ever loved or was likely to love anyone, yet he couldn't be physically close to her, even though every fibre in his being wanted to at least let his arm be a pillow for her head, so that he could run his fingers through her hair while she dreamed her dreams.

Her mouth had slightly opened. Joseph smiled. She shifted about a bit. The resultant displacement of her T-shirt had exposed a couple of inches of her slim brown waist, and Joseph, who had mostly heterosexual bones in his body, couldn't help but stare. With a start, he noticed that Aastha's eyes had opened and she was looking at him with a caught-you smile.

'Would you like to sleep in the kitchen?' she said.

'Eh—er—uh—no, I'm okay here. I'll just—close my eyes and sleep.'

And so Joseph turned away and closed his eyes. She looked so very pure while sleeping, he thought. The one thing that made the whole universe make sense, the solitary objective towards which all his life's actions were geared. Joseph's plan was to wait until Aastha was well and truly in Morpheus territory, then again stare at her lovely face.

Unfortunately, he fell asleep within a minute.

Two days later, Joseph found himself staring at Arjun Pathania's name on the door of a vanity van in a studio lot in Film City. Tonmoy knocked and a deep voice told them to come in.

On his laptop, Arjun Pathania was watching a show where a stand-up comedian was cracking a joke about his National Award.

'Asshole,' muttered Arjun Pathania.

'Hi, Arjun,' said Tonmoy. 'This is my college friend Joseph. He's a great guitarist.'

'Hi, Joseph,' said Pathania, offering his hand.

'Hi Arjun. Nice to meet you. Can't say I'm a very big fan of your acting, but I've always admired you as an ideal manly man.'

Pathania smiled and said thanks.

'I've got a bit of an unusual request,' said Joseph.

'What is it?'

'My girlfriend's dying and one of her last wishes is a date with you.'

It was a deadpan look that Pathania cast at Joseph, as though he was trying to figure out if someone was pulling a fast one on him.

'Nice guy,' said Joseph as they stepped out of the van ten minutes later. 'Er... does he have the reputation of being a womaniser?'

'Not that I know of. The only person who's ever said anything on those lines was Uma, and as we all know, she's one hell of a bitch.'

'What did she say?'

'That he had made a pass at her.'

'Hah! In her dreams! Ridd-diculous! With beauties revolving around him 24/7, why da health would he go for Uma, of all people?'

'The only person who'd make a pass at her would be one of my ex-bosses, who had a thing for plump women... But listen, is she really dying?'

'Uma?'

'Of course not, although that's not an unpleasant thought. I mean your girl.'

Joseph nodded.

'Shit! You serious?'

'Yeah.'

'Shit. Dammit. Such a nice girl.' Tonmoy looked like *he* was going to cry. Joseph put an arm around his shoulder and said, 'Calm down; don't get so emotional. And please do not, do not, do not tell anybody. We don't want anyone behaving weirdly around her.'

Oriental Heaven in Lokhandwala was chosen as the venue for Aastha's date with Arjun Pathania. Joseph's mood started its downward slide the moment he and Aastha stepped into their auto. Probably one in a million chaps had the misfortune to arrange a date for the girl he loved with another man. By the time they stepped into the restaurant, Joseph was as cheerful as Othello at the climactic moment where he says words to the effect of 'Oh crap! What've I done!'

He was hoping that Pathania would behave in such a snooty starry manner that Aastha would be put off even before the starters and appetisers and make for the nearest exit.

But no such thing happened. Pathania had already reached the place before them, and he stood up with a charming smile as he said hi and shook hands with Aastha, who was grinning ear to ear like the schoolgirl she had been when she had developed a huge crush on the man who was now in front of her.

'Joseph didn't tell me you were so pretty,' said Pathania.

Aastha practically blushed. Joseph looked at her and said, 'I suppose that goes without saying.'

'Well, sit down, sit down.'

As Aastha sat, Joseph said, 'I think I'll leave now. Don't wanna be the kabab mein haddi.'

'Don't be silly,' said Pathania.

Aastha put a hand on Joseph's arm and said, 'Stay, why don't you.'

'This is your dream moment. I don't wanna intrude.'

'Oh, come on.'

'No really, it's fine.' Then he said to Pathania, 'I'll see if I can manage dinner with Sushmita Sen.'

'Ha ha ha. Well, good luck then,' said Pathania.

'Catch you later,' said Joseph to Aastha.

'Yup,' she said, and as she looked at him, both of them knew there was something different in each other's eyes this time.

Joseph walked out of the restaurant feeling the weirdest he had felt in his life. He was simultaneously happy that he had fulfilled Aastha's third wish and torn because, well, it involved a grand dinner with another bloke she had had, and obviously still had a crush on. Barely registering his own actions, he waved down an auto and got in.

Back at Nadia's place, Joseph sat on the couch in the hall and picked up *Maxim* magazine to get his mind off Aastha and Arjun Pathania.

He had just turned to a picture of a seminude model when the front door flew open and Nadia stormed in. Joseph quickly discarded the magazine and stammered a hi.

'Hi,' said Nadia on autopilot. Then she hurled her bag onto the floor. Thump! She looked angry and close to tears. Joseph wasn't sure whether she was the kind who preferred to be left alone or who would want someone to talk to. Taking the polite option, he asked, 'What's the matter?'

Nadia didn't answer right away. She started searching the cabinets and shelves for something, muttering, 'Asshole sonofabitch liar bastard bloody pig...'

'Er—who?' said Joseph when there was a lull in the tide of abuse.

Nadia found what she was looking for—a half bottle of whisky. She took a glass and mixed herself a strong one.

'I thought you didn't drink?' said Joseph.

'Today's a good day to start,' said Nadia as she took a long draught.

'What happened?'

Nadia made a face as the alcohol stung her oesophagus. 'What did he think? Bombay's such a big place that I'd never see him? I was right there on the first floor when he was coochie-cooing with that bitch across the table!'

'Your—ex-boyfriend?'

'Well, he certainly *is* my *ex*-boyfriend now.'

'Gaurav?'

'Don't even take that mother-'s name in front of me. Filthy stray dog looking for bitches! Kutta saala harami!'

Joseph tried to find the appropriate thing to say. The best he could come up with was, 'There might be some kind of misunderstanding. Not everything is what it looks like.'

'Really? How about slowwwwly sliding his finger on her arm and then holding her hand!'

Nadia took another swig to wash down the painful image.

For Joseph, it was as if the visual Nadia had just described transferred itself to his brain, but with a different pair of principal players. An image suddenly flashed into his mind's eye: Arjun Pathania slowwwwly sliding his finger along Aastha's arm and then holding her hand. The scene jolted Joseph.

Nadia continued. 'Then the dog crossed over and sat beside the bitch and put his stinking arm around her waist! What d'you think? They were rehearsing a love scene?'

Another image flashed into Joseph's brain: Arjun Pathania putting his arm around Aastha's waist!

Joseph literally gasped. He looked at Nadia's glass and said, 'May I?'

Nadia absentmindedly handed him the glass. Joseph absentmindedly took it and downed a long sip. Grimacing, he handed it back while Nadia continued her sordid story.

'Then he kissed that bitch! On the lips! In public!'

Saas-bahu cymbals started crashing in Joseph's ears. Were it not for the disturbing visions inflicting themselves on him, he would have thought of saying that not everything was what it looked like, then he would have reasoned, correctly, that such a remark would lead to Nadia bringing the whisky bottle down on his skull just like her friend Aastha had once brought a hammer down on a laptop.

Instead, he immediately suffered the shocking vision of Arjun Pathania holding Aastha by the waist, about to kiss her on the lips... ! In public!

'Stop!' said Joseph.

'Eh?' said Nadia, who was pouring herself another one.

'I mean,' said Joseph, snapping back to reality, 'uh, may I have another sip?'

While Joseph sipped, Nadia ranted. 'Then that sonofabitch walked to the bitch's car with his arm around her waist. And I think they were smooching as they drove off...'

Ominous trumpets and bass notes and cymbals started playing in Joseph's head as his mind's eye saw Arjun Pathania lead a smiling Aastha to his car. Fortunately for Joseph, this ghastly vision was interrupted by a more immediate minor crisis: Nadia had started sobbing.

She covered her face with her hands and slumped down onto the sofa beside him. Not finding her own hands adequate, she picked up a cushion and sobbed into it, making for a very tragicomic sight.

Joseph didn't know what to do. They'd become friends over the past two days; he'd grown to like her and was genuinely sorry that she was crying, but what on earth was the right course of consolatory action for him? Should he say 'Everything's gonna be all right'? He personally felt like punching people who used that line on him in tragic times, so he didn't think too much of it. Should he proffer his shoulder for her to cry on? Should he put an arm around her shoulder? Were they already that close or did the circumstances dictate that they get close? Oh, tough!

He decided an arm around her shoulder *might* just be the decent thing to do. Awkwardly, nervously, he extended his arm when bzzt—his hand touched her bare shoulder and he immediately retracted. She was wearing a spaghetti strap top, and Joseph—not having been with a woman in nearly a year—wasn't too sure whether his touch would be purely platonic and devoid of any feelings of the flesh, so to speak.

In a pre-emptive move, Nadia suddenly planted her face, still cushion-covered, on Joseph's shoulder, and continued sobbing. Well, he thought, it certainly wouldn't be too polite to just sit still and play a detached Sphinx-like observer. He took a deep breath, mustered some courage and then firmly put an arm around her shoulder.

The rebound effect strongly affects most people who've been recently jilted. They tend to latch on to the first mildly eligible interested person around, out of either desperation or revenge. Furthermore, some say that the moments immediately after a spell of grief are rife with physical arousal.

It might have been either one, or both, or neither of these two factors that came into play, but Nadia's free arm suddenly wrapped itself around Joseph's shoulder.

Joseph looked at Nadia's hand on his shoulder. If he held it or patted it, would it be condescending? Comforting? Chance pe dance?

Without analysing any further, he put his hand on Nadia's. She stiffened slightly. Then she raised her head off the cushion.

They were staring into each other's eyes now. Something was happening. Their faces drew closer… closer… closer…

Swish! Both of them simultaneously turned away, just inches away from first contact.

Hyperactive Imagination 207

Ahem ahem. Nadia started fixing her hair. Joseph did some unnecessary things with his collar, then he noticed his T-shirt didn't have one.

'I think I'll get some fresh air,' he said, standing up.

'Yup,' said Nadia quickly without looking at him.

Joseph rapidly walked out the door. He rapidly walked back in.

'Er, is there a wine shop nearby?'

'Go left from the gate and take the second left from there.'

'Okay.'

'Aastha said you didn't drink.'

Joseph had another flash: Arjun Pathania showing Aastha his bedroom!

He blinked hard and said to Nadia, 'Today's a good day to start.'

The actual reality of Aastha's dinner with Arjun Pathania was in stark contrast to Joseph's morbid imaginings. Conversation was civil, both parties were at their charming best, and the only attempt at being fresh—a successful one, at that—was made by the salad. Pathania was a thorough gentleman.

'Which of your films are you most embarrassed by?' asked Aastha over dessert—blueberry cheesecake with hot chocolate fudge.

'Ha ha ha. That's a tough one—excuse me a sec.' Pathania checked a message on his cell, then said,

'Y'know, I've never met someone who knew they were about to—well, y'know—and were still so serene and yet full of life... Is there anything special I can do for you?'

'Um... This dinner is already that special thing.'

'Oh come on.'

'No, really... But there's something you could do for Joseph. He's really talented. Composes great songs. If you could help introduce him to the right people...'

'Yeah, sure. I'll do that.'

'Thanks. That'd be wonderful. He comes up with lovely things on the guitar.'

'Well, I'm sure he plays it better than me. I'm just an actor.'

'I think he's a better actor too—oops, I mean—wrong thing to say.'

'Ha ha ha, that's okay. I don't have any delusions of grandeur.'

'But of course, you're infinitely more handsome. I mean, I don't think there's anyone better-looking and better-sounding than you. And you're such a gentleman.'

'Thanks for all the praise. Hope I can live up to it.'

As they waited for Pathania's car outside the restaurant, their eyes met.

'What is it?' he asked.

'Can I say something weird?'

'As long as you remember that I'm married.'

'Yes, I know,' said Aastha with a slightly embarrassed chuckle. 'It's just—well, I've been a fan for ten years. I used to think that if I ever met you I would—I mean, if you tried, that is—I would let you seduce me.'

Aastha's childhood crush laughed merrily.

'Silly, I know,' she said.

'No, no, it's kind of sweet—in its own twisted way.'

'But the funny thing is—right now, the most dominant thought in my mind isn't our dinner together, but rather, the desire to tell all about it to—Joseph.'

'I think you're a lucky couple.'

'Only—we're not yet a couple.'

'Well, what're you waiting for?'

Aastha thought for a moment, then said, 'I knew the answer at some point of time. I just don't remember what it was anymore.'

The car arrived.

Twenty minutes later, they were at the gate of Nadia's housing society.

'Well, it was nice meeting you,' said Pathania. 'Gave me some perspective.'

'Thanks for meeting me. And for dinner.'

Pathania leaned over and gave Aastha a peck on the cheek. She blushed invisibly.

'Well, uh,' she said, 'thanks for that too'.

'Don't forget to remove the lipstick from your cheek.'

Puzzled for an instant, Aastha raised a hand to her cheek, then got the joke and chuckled.

'Bye,' she said, opening the car door.

'Goodbye, Aastha.'

And a minute later he was out of sight.

Aastha stood still for a moment, letting it sink in that what had just happened wasn't just a dream. She had actually met her childhood crush and had a wonderful time with him. Then her thoughts drifted to the boy who had made this possible—who had stuck with her all this time, even going to the extent of facilitating a date with another man, when he was probably feeling crushed himself.

Joseph, I'm coming.

She ran up the four flights of stairs to Nadia's door and hit the bell. The door was opened by a drowsy Nadia, who had cried and drunk herself to sleep.

'Are you all right? Sleeping already?'

'Hm,' murmured Nadia, trying to get a grip on shapes and sounds.

'Where's Joseph?'

Nadia put together a few recollections and said, 'I think he went to get some booze.'

'Booze? Joseph? Where?'

She got directions from Nadia and rushed out, taking the stairs again instead of waiting for the lift. She took long, fast strides, scanning the footpaths and corners for her missing almost-boyfriend. Half a dozen stray dogs watched with lazily sympathetic eyes while three others followed her, briefly mistaking her for the actress who used to come around at night and feed them biscuits. A few customers were having omelettes at an anda-pavwala. Futher on, a pirated-DVD salesman was packing up for the day, possibly unaware of the many curses film producers and exhibitors had heaped on his ilk over the last twenty-four hours.

She took the second left and found herself on a quiet street with a huge, posh-looking residential complex on one side and a posh-looking school on the other. The street was well lit, the weather was pleasant with a light breeze blowing, and several people were taking their post-dinner walks. A solitary girl was talking on her cell, obviously with a new boyfriend. A few boys sat around on their bikes. Where was he?

There! In a distant corner, slightly obscured by a tree, he sat, a bottle of vodka and a pack of cranberry juice by his side and a half-empty plastic glass in his hand. He was staring at the ground.

She crept up behind him and grabbed his neck. Joseph received a pint-sized heart attack and the remaining drink fell out of the glass.

'Good God! It's you.'
'Who'd you think?'
'I thought it was the local witch or bhatakti aatma.'

Aastha had a flashback. 'You're in the same position I found you the first time we met. Sitting with a plastic glass in hand, despondent.'

'How'd it go?'

'Well. He's quite a gentleman... How come you're drinking?'

She knew the answer, but wanted to hear his version. He wasn't looking at her.

'My, my, jealous Joseph,' said Aastha, and burst out laughing. She sat down with an arm around him. 'We didn't do anything.'

'What d'you mean?'

'He just gave me a peck on the cheek while dropping me off. That's all.'

'That's all?' said Joseph, meeting her gaze at last. 'He didn't hold your waist or make seductive bedroom eyes at you or mentally undress you or anything? You can tell me the truth, y'know. Like I said, I'd rather have the ugly truth than a bed of lies.'

Aastha almost laughed her guts out. 'Oh God! You have such a hyperactive imagination. I don't know if he mentally undressed me—I don't think he did—but he definitely didn't make bedroom eyes.'

Joseph looked into Aastha's eyes and saw she was obviously telling it like it had happened. He finally relaxed and allowed himself a relieved sigh. 'Well, I guess not all film stars are horny old bastards.'

'So can we go home now?'

'... He really didn't try anything?'

'No.'

'Oh, wonderful. Now help me up, please.'

Aastha lifted Joseph to his feet and they started homeward.

'How does it feel to be drunk?' she asked.

'Useless. Why da health do people drink? My head's feeling light—or is it heavy? But I don't feel like singing songs aloud or dancing naked in the streets. And it doesn't even taste good.'

Back in the flat, Aastha gently prodded Nadia awake and asked, 'Hey babe, is Gaurav gonna be late tonight?'

'He's not coming back tonight,' said a very groggy Nadia.

'Why?'

'I'll tell you tomorrow.'

'Okay. Sleep.'

In the hall, Joseph was splayed out on the mattress, two winks away from forty winks.

'Aren't you gonna brush before sleeping?' said Aastha.

'I do my second brushing at teatime. I'm too sleepy now.'

'Please brush.'

'Why? Let me sleep.'

'We need to talk.'

Joseph's antenna went up instantly. In his previous relationships, those four words had always been the harbinger of doom for the day, inevitably followed as they were by accusations and complaints. He wondered what he could possibly have done wrong. Oh, of course, he had tried to drown his sorrows in drink.

'What about?' he asked guardedly. Then he noticed that Aastha had a flirtatious smile on her face.

'Shut up and brush.'

So Joseph hurriedly brushed. As he wiped his face, he asked, 'So what did you want to talk about?'

Aastha looked into his eyes in a way she never had before, then said, 'Thanks for making all my wishes come true.'

'Oh you don't have to thank mmfff—'

Aastha had held his face and planted her lips right on his. A long, passionate, loving kiss followed.

To say that Joseph was shell-shocked would be an understatement. For a full ten seconds after that wholly unexpected kiss, he was left wondering what had happened. Then it dawned on him that this wasn't a dream, and the girl he loved had actually kissed him. He smiled a smile wild horses couldn't have pulled down. Then they embraced. Then they looked into each other's eyes. Then she suddenly slapped him!

'Ow! What was that?' said Joseph, stunned by the bipolar behaviour.

Aastha held his face again, tenderly this time, and said, 'Why didn't you ask my name nine years ago?'

Joseph smiled, put his arms around Aastha's waist, and said, 'I've asked myself that question again and again. And I haven't been able to find a good answer, except maybe that I was just plain stupid not to recognise a good thing when I saw it.'

'Never mind. No point complaining over what I don't or didn't have. I'd rather celebrate what I do have.'

She kissed him again. They sat down on the makeshift bed. For about a minute, they just sat silently, looking at each other. Joseph broke the silence.

'How was your dinner?'

'To hell with my dinner. Tell me about yourself. Tell me some dirty little secret.'

'Dirty little secret?... Well, let's see... In school, I frequently used to stare at my Social Studies teacher's bust. I realise now that it must've been very obvious to her because I used to sit on the first bench, and it's pretty embarrassing in hindsight.'

Aastha laughed. 'What about me? Have you ever—stared at me?'

'I do it all the time. I mean—not at your bust—which is of course ahem—well formed too—but you're beautiful—all of you. I can't help staring.'

'Beautiful? I don't usually get that. Pretty, yes. Slim, yes. Beautiful, almost never.'

'You're everything. I don't know how to properly explain this. After I get to know a person properly, I somehow seem to see them as a combination of their physical appearance and their internal qualities as well. A not-so-hot girl, if I get to know her to be a really wonderful person, somehow starts looking prettier to me.'

'Hm. Would you say I'm hot?'

Joseph thought for a second and said, 'Let me put it this way: you make me happy that I'm not gay. Not that—in the words of Jerry Seinfeld—there's anything wrong with it.'

Another smile played on Aastha's face. 'Do you have protection?'

Joseph was taken aback, but he tried to play it cool. 'Um, there's one in my wallet. But it's been there for a year now. I could go and get a new one—ones.'

'No need. It'll be okay.'

'You're obviously not a virgin, I guess?'

'What if I'm not?'

'Good if you're not. I don't want to be the one to cause you all the pain of inauguration.'

'My ribbon has already been cut.'

'Eugh. How vulgar.'

Aastha sniggered and said, '"Inauguration" isn't an appetising term either.'

'What if Nadia wakes up?'

'We'll ask her to join us, ha ha ha…'

And so the boy and the girl finally made love…

'What're you thinking?' she asked later as they lay in each other's arms.

'Trying to reconcile two contradictory philosophies. "Today is the first day of the rest of your life." "Live every day like it's your last." '

'I'm trying to reconcile two contradictory impulses, too.'

'What?'

' "I want to drink water." "I just want to lie down here." '

'I'll get it.'

'Thank you so much.'

'No problemo, madamo.'

Joseph fished around in the dark but his undies were the only thing that surfaced in his hands. He put them on. 'Where are my shorts?'

'Never mind. Just go quickly.'

Joseph gingerly walked the few steps to the kitchen. There was just enough of a combination of moonlight and streetlight to make out a waterbottle next to the microwave. As he picked it up, the kitchen light suddenly came on. Standing with her finger on the switch was not Aastha, but Nadia!

'Aiee!' was the short shriek from Nadia. '… Oh, it's you.'

Although it goes without saying, a point to be noted, your honour, is that Joseph was supremely embarrassed. Standing in your hostess' kitchen in your underwear—no matter of what superior quality—with a bottle of water in hand is not the ideal situation to be seen in by her.

The forthcoming description is sequential, but the events themselves were simultaneous. Joseph said oh, sorry. Nadia said my God, sorry. She reached for the light switch but in her haste ended up turning on the fan instead. Oh, sorry, she said again. Then she hit the correct switch and the light went off.

'I—I just came for some water,' stuttered Joseph.

'Uh—me too,' said Nadia.

She opened the fridge door and the bulb inside lit up, again illuminating Joseph, who was still standing there, looking almost like the statue of David except for the nudity not being full frontal, and the waterbottle, and the yellow-brown tinge. Nadia hurriedly extracted a bottle of water, shut the fridge and went into her room without another word. Both of them could hear Aastha cackling in the hall.

'So did she drool at the sight of you?' said Aastha when Joseph was back with her.

'Shuddup. She just wanted some water.'

'Hmmm... pyaasi ladki...'

'Shaadaap,' he said, reaching for her throat.

Joseph stirred. It was morning. He opened his eyes to a pleasant surprise—last night hadn't been just a dream—Aastha was lying next to him. She was already awake, and looking at him.

'Morning,' said Joseph, putting an arm around her waist.

'Mm-hm,' mumbled Aastha. Then she signalled 'one minute', and got up.

She brushed her teeth, then came back and lay down beside him again.

'Good morning,' she said brightly.

'You brushed just to say that?'

'Never understood how people in Hollywood flicks wake up and kiss straight away—what with all that morning breath. Ew.'

Joseph took the hint. He pulled himself up and went to brush.

'Good morning,' he said when he was done, sitting beside her once again.

Then he noticed she was looking uneasy. Her head was drooping.

'I'm suddenly feeling cold,' she said.

Alarm bells went off in Joseph's head. 'I'll call an ambulance!'

'There's no need for an ambulance,' said Aastha firmly. 'An auto will do. I'm not gonna die. Just feeling a little out of sorts.'

Joseph hurriedly put on his clothes, asked Nadia to help Aastha with hers, then rushed out for an auto.

'Nothing serious,' said Dr Mokashe, checking the drip rate of the IV hooked up to Aastha's wrist. 'Just low BP. You can take her home after a couple of hours,' he said to Joseph and Nadia.

'Thanks, sir,' said Joseph. 'There's really nothing seriously wrong, right?'

The salt-and-pepper-bearded doctor looked at Joseph meaningfully, then said, 'Not as of now, no.' Joseph had previously taken him aside and told him of Aastha's condition.

'Okay. Thanks.'

'You are her—?'

'Um—boyfriend.'

Dr Mokashe smiled and exited into the corridor. Joseph followed him and said, 'Er, doctor, one more thing.'

'Yeah?'

Joseph lowered his voice and said, 'We, er, we were together last night. Does that have anything to do with this?'

'You didn't do anything extraordinary, did you?'

Joseph needed a few seconds to place the question in context, because for him, last night *had* been extraordinary.

'Um—by "extraordinary" you mean... ?'

'You're not into S&M and bondage type stuff, are you?'

'Eh? God, no. Just the usual. I mean—last night was our first time together.'

'Was it her first time?'

'No.'

'Then it's okay. Shouldn't have anything to do with that... She's not trying to be a model or actress, is she?'

'Eh? No. Why?'

'Just thought she might be one of those trying to hit size sub-zero.'

'Oh, no, not at all,' said Joseph.

'Just make sure she eats well.'

'Oh, that she does. She eats very well,' said Joseph, grinning at the memory of Aastha's thirteenth momo.

'Good,' said Dr Mokashe, and excused himself.

Aastha woke up an hour later and said, 'I'm hungry.'

Fifteen minutes later, she had eaten and almost all was well with the world again.

Nadia went out to take a call. Seizing this chance for privacy, Joseph fished in his wallet and took out a piece of paper. He said, 'There's something I need to tell you. I wrote this down in case something happened to me before you—like an accident or something.'

Aastha put her hand on Joseph's mouth and very filmily said, 'Na re saiyyan, aisa na bolo.'

'Shuddup,' said Joseph, half cracking up. 'Since the deal was that I couldn't tell you what my feelings for you were, I decided a couple of months ago to let them out on paper instead. But I think circumstances changed last night. So here goes...'

Joseph unfolded the letter. Aastha said, 'Ahem.'

'Don't crack jokes, okay,' said Joseph. Aastha put a finger on her lips.

'Aastha, I'm writing this after fifty days together. It goes without saying that these fifty days have been the best of my life. It's been wonderful. But it's also been agonising because it looks like my silly little theory about soulmates seems to be turning out true. All the things that should be happening with true love are happening. You complete me, you make me wanna be a better man etcetera etcetera… Oh screw this,' said Joseph, putting the letter down. 'It's too mushy. Read it yourself later.'

Aastha took the letter and said, 'Why later?' Then she proceeded to read it, smiling all the while with an occasional giggle.

When it was done, she stretched out her arms. They embraced and kissed.

Then Joseph held her hand and said, 'The doctor asked me what I am to you.'

'Hm?'

'I said boyfriend, but I want to be able to give a different answer next time someone asks.'

'What?'

Joseph got down on his knees. The trouble was, the hospital bed was too high and only his face was visible above it; he looked like a dwarf.

'Sit beside me,' said Aastha.

'Right. This is awkward.'

So he sat beside her, held her hand and then said:

'I wanted to say—I don't care if it's just for a few years or even just for one day. I want the honour of being able to say in the—hopefully distant—future that I was once your husband. That I was once married to the most wonderful girl in the world.'

Aastha smiled her widest smile for a few seconds before saying, 'Your father won't ask for any dowry, will he?'

'No, he won't.'

'I'm—free next weekend. Shall we get married then?'

It was Joseph's turn to smile his widest. 'Sure. Why delay?' And they embraced again.

'Ahem!' It was a nurse who had just entered. 'Sir, please don't sit on the patient's bed.'

Chapter 19

Making Memories

AND SO THE BOY AND THE GIRL GOT MARRIED IN THE VERY same church where they had first met. She wore a beautiful white gown gifted by her new stepmother. He wore a brand-new black suit gifted by his only mother. It was a simple ceremony with only close friends and family invited, eschewing the usual practice of inviting even people who couldn't care less whether one was getting married or having a vasectomy.

As they took their wedding vows, the girl's father was happy that his little girl had found new happiness—not that she was unhappy before—but it also tore him up inside that it might not last as long as they would all have liked it to. He was stoutly holding back his tears when he heard someone already sobbing and sniffing beside him—it was Utpal. He gave him a smile and a pat on the back.

When the pastor pronounced them husband and wife, their friends loudly cheered and applauded. 'Kiss the bride! Kiss the bride!' shouted the ones who had seen many Hollywood films.

'Should I?' he asked her.

'Make it short. We don't wanna scandalise our elders.'

And so he planted a quick kiss on her lips. The whoops and cheers increased.

Winter was almost over, but the wedding provided a perfect excuse for a bonfire during the feast at her place that night. Those so inclined roasted pork and potatoes in the fire. The mothers and fathers did most of the cooking and the sons and daughters and friends did most of the overeating. Guitars were played and songs were sung till one in the night. The most repeated song was Matt Nathanson's *Wedding Dress*, which Joseph insisted was actually about divorce, even though he loved the song too.

When the last guests had left, Joseph's father came up to him and said, 'Where's Ma?'

Joseph found his mother and Nadia fast asleep in Aastha's bed. She'd likely crossed her drinking-without-falling-asleep number of drinks.

'Ma! Wake up.'

It was Nadia who stirred first.

'Oops, sorry, Nadia,' said Joseph. 'Go back to sleep.'

'Sorry I fell asleep. I'm kind of jetlagged,' said Nadia, then closed her eyes again.

'Ma!'

'Hmm...' murmured Joseph's mother through half-open eyes. 'You've got school today?'

'No,' said Joseph with a smile, as he gently propped her up. 'I got married today.'

'Oh, right. Congratulations, son,' she said and kissed him on the cheek. Then she saw that her dressing table had suddenly changed shape, size, colour and location, and so had the bed, and someone had painted the walls overnight. Then the realisation dawned upon her that she was in someone else's room. 'Oh. I fell asleep.'

'Yeah. Come, let's go now.'

Joseph's parents left for an uncle's place and Utpal went to drop Nadia off at her parents'.

'So, where d'you want to stay tonight?' Mr Mishra asked Aastha as they watched Joseph put out the fire. Then he answered the question himself. 'Actually, go and stay with your husband. It's your wedding night. Come back tomorrow morning for breakfast.'

Aastha looked at her father and said mischievously, 'I guess you too could use the privacy.'

'Badtameez!'

She ducked before he could grab her ear.

So Aastha went with Joseph to his apartment.

'Let's do the carrying-up-the-stairs thing,' he said, and lifted her in his arms without waiting for an answer.

They washed and changed and settled under a blanket.

'Do people really have any energy left to do anything on their suhaag raat?' said Joseph.

'Good thing we've already had ours.'

Then they fell asleep.

Two weeks later, they headed to Tawang, the most beautiful place for a honeymoon. Postcard-worthy locations and sights are abundant once you start climbing the hills. Waterfalls, big and small, are so numerous that one feels like protesting the unfairness of it all and demanding that the government move some of them to whichever congested polluted city one comes from. Landslides, though, are an occasional hazard during the rainy season.

They stayed the night in Bomdila, where they had mithun momos—not momos made by the disco-dancing actor, but momos made with the meat of the mithun, a cousin of the buffalo.

The next night was spent in Dirang, a small but picturesque town, like almost all of Arunachal Pradesh's. A few kilometres from there was a famous hot spring, which they visited after breakfast.

In the afternoon they went to the Gompa, which was built on top of a hill with a wonderful panoramic view of the surroundings. On one side was a valley with a river running through it in the distance. On the other side were huge hills completely covered in green except for a small occasional brown speck where a house stood. The constant breeze kept the colourful flags of the temple fluttering all the time.

'This place is heaven, isn't it?' said Aastha as they sat on the grass and took in the view. Joseph nodded.

'This world is hell, isn't it?' said Joseph to the statue of the Buddha inside the Gompa, when Aastha was at a distance admiring the murals.

The Buddha didn't reply. Joseph continued his muted monologue. 'We're taught that if we're good, we'll go to heaven, and if we're bad, we'll go to hell. But what if this world itself is actually hell? We're actually already in it? Never mind about me and Aastha. What kind of world is it in which innocent little children get abused and disfigured and killed? This has to be hell.'

Joseph looked over his shoulder. Aastha was outside. Then he went on. 'I'll tell you why else I think this world is hell. She's the nicest, greatest girl in the world and you want to take her away quickly. Why?'Cause you don't want her to suffer anymore? That must mean that *this* world is hell.

'Okay, now let me be selfish for a minute. I doubt I'm ever gonna find anyone like her ever again. I know I don't pray or do anything of that kind, but I've never done anyone any harm. Isn't that better than praying in the morning and beating your wife at night?'

Then Joseph did something he hadn't done in sixteen years. He got down on his knees to pray.

'Yes, I'm being selfish, but I'm asking you for a miracle. Please, please do something, anything. Let her stay with me for at least another thirty years. I know only one person's lived beyond her age with that disease, but there's a first time for everything. Or second. And you can do it if you want. Please, don't take her away. Let her be one of your rare miracles. Please.'

'You're praying?'

Aastha had materialised behind him.

'Not at all.'

She took his hand and they walked out.

One of the most heavenly aspects of going to Tawang is that above a certain altitude, you can see the clouds literally below you. On some stretches, they look like a huge blanket of cotton that stretches all the way to the horizon. They look so inviting, one is tempted to exclaim 'Yipeeeee!' and take a swan dive into all that cotton, except that actually doing so would lead to a free fall of around ten thousand feet, if not interrupted by hills and rocky mountainsides on the way down, and the 'Yipeeeee!' would turn into a long 'Yaaaaaaaa.......!', followed by crunch! Squish! Splat!

The Sela Pass is the second highest motorable road in the world. The newlyweds stopped at a tiny restaurant built on the edge of the hillside next to the official gate. They ate Maggi and tried a shot of rum to keep their bones from freezing.

They visited the Jaswantgarh temple and spent some time at the majestic Jung falls before finally reaching Tawang in the afternoon.

They tried yak momos in the evening, which is when Aastha felt dizziness and an agonising pain in her abdomen. She doubled over on the ground, pounding it with her fists. Joseph yelled for someone to get them a taxi or something.

'Let's go home,' said Joseph in the hospital.

'Nonsense. Why would anyone come here and not spend at least a few days? I'm feeling better.'

The doctor had administered a painkilling injection, but Joseph knew it was only a temporary remedy. He had read enough to know what the signs were...

That night in the hotel, at bedtime, while Joseph washed up in the bathroom, Aastha pulled apart a green-white medicine capsule, poured its contents into a small waterbottle and shook it vigorously.

'Get the guitar. I wanna sing,' she said, sitting up in bed and wrapping herself up in blankets.

'Just a sec.'

Joseph took the bottle and drank half the water. Aastha watched.

'Okay, what d'you wanna sing?'

'Gimme B sus.'

Joseph strummed B sus and Aastha began singing one of their songs. Her voice had a hint of sadness which Joseph interpreted as exhaustion. They sang another four songs, two their own, then Sarah McLachlan's *I Will Remember You* and *Falling Slowly* by Glen Hansard and Marketa Irglova, before Aastha called it a night.

'I'm feeling sleepy too,' said Joseph.

They lay down face to face.

'G'night, love,' said Joseph, and kissed her.

'Good night, my good knight. And thanks for everything.'

'Don't say thanks.'

'Okay, I won't say it again, but this is the second last time: thanks for everything.'

'You're welcome. When's the last gonna be?'

'Later.'

He was soon asleep. She looked at his face for a long time, then sat up. She took her mobile and pressed the camera button.

Ten minutes later, she opened her skybag and extracted a plastic medicine bottle from a corner. It was almost full with the same green-white capsules.

She looked back. Joseph was in deep sleep. She turned away, took a deep breath, then took a handful of the capsules, put them in her mouth, and washed them down with water. Then she took another handful.

When the bottle was empty, she poured herself a glass of the extremely tasty local maize wine they had tried after dinner and really liked. She sat at the head of the bed, said cheers to her sleeping loved one, then started sipping the wine.

A little later, the wine was finished. He was facing the other way. With a bit of grunt-inducing effort, she rolled him over to face her. Then she lay down beside him and pulled up the blankets. She put one hand on his face, gave him a long kiss, then said: 'Thanks for everything… I'll always love you.'

She thought she saw a slight twitch of his lips, as though he was trying for a smile of acknowledgement through his sleep. She smiled and kissed him again, then took his arm and put it around her.

Her eyelids involuntarily blinked. She could feel them getting heavy.

It was morning once again. Joseph stirred. He scrunched his brow. Headache? He rolled over and saw Aastha was lying with her back towards him.

He reached out a hand and touched her waist. His hand went cold, and then his feet. He reached out with a now trembling hand and touched her bare arm. It was completely cold.

He sat up. Turned her over. Touched her face. Cold. He placed a finger under her nose. Nothing. He tried to listen for a heartbeat. Nothing again.

He took several long, long, breaths to restrain himself. He cradled her in his arms and looked at her face. She looked peaceful.

He sat that way for a long time, just looking at her. He would never hear her sing again, nor would she ever again punch his arm and say shut up, stupid, nor would she ever stuff an empty chocolate wrapper into his pocket.

After an eternity, the realisation dawned that he had to do something. He slowly got up and covered her.

Like a zombie, he walked into the bathroom, picked up his brush, applied toothpaste, and started brushing.

After he had cleaned himself up, he drank some water, then picked up her cell and dialled her father's number.

'Good morning, beta.'

'... Er, no, Uncle—it's—it's me.'

'Is... is everything all right?'

He couldn't answer. His sharp, heavy breathing gave it away. He could hear her father starting to break down.

He played the video message she had recorded for him in her final minutes. She smiled as she spoke.

'Joseph, I'm sorry for doing this. I know it's going to be a big mess for you, but this is the fourth task—my last wish, which I've made you grant without your consent... I wanted to quit while I'm really happy, not while I'm in pain. I wanted the goodbye to happen in your arms, not in some ICU surrounded by nurses and tubes and machines. I wanted to leave you while you were smiling, not wallowing in the tragedy of me dying in agony. I'm being selfish, yes. I don't want to go through a painful death, but I don't want you or Papa to go through all that either. I had decided long long ago that I wouldn't go out in a long lingering manner. I had a prescription for these sleeping pills, and I've been collecting them for a long time now.'

She paused to look at him, then said with a chuckle, 'You either die a heroine or live long enough to see yourself become the vamp. I don't know. What I do know now is that as I leave you at this moment, we love each other at the rate of hundred per cent—hey that rhymes… Anyway, I hope you understand. I really, really love you and I'll thank God for sending you to make my last days so very happy. I don't think I have any regrets. I just hope that reincarnation does happen and that I get a second chance with you… As for this life, move to Mumbai. You'll be able to do much more there with your talents.

'Despite my best efforts not to, I fell in love with you. I've seen many boys, but there's never been one as angelic and sensitive as you. Maybe you're actually a woman's spirit wearing men's underwear,' she said and chortled once more. 'But whatever, I love you…

'You told me at the beginning that you didn't like secrets. Well, I've got two final secrets. One is in my email account. The password is a-l-j-@-100%, which means Aastha loves Joseph at the rate of 100 per cent. Silly, I know. But do check it out. It's important.'

A solitary tear had appeared on her face. She wiped it away and said, 'I have to say goodbye now. I wish we could have had more time together, but I want to do this while I still can, before I lose my dignity and volition. So, goodbye, my love. I love you. I always will. And I promise I'll plead before God to bring us together in our next life. If he refuses, I'll kick his divine ass... Bye bye. I love you. Be happy and have a wonderful life.'

The video ended. Struggling not to fall totally apart, he put down the cell and looked at the shrouded form of his love on the bed.

Chapter 20

The End

She was buried in the graveyard of the same church in which they had first met and also got married.

Remarkably, he had managed to keep in check the storm brewing inside all the way back to their city and till the time of the funeral. After she had been laid to rest and her grave had been filled in, he knelt and placed a single red rose on it. He looked at the church and remembered the very first time he had heard her voice... singing gloriously. This was almost the same place where he had been standing then.

His parents stood by his side while he stared unseeingly at the grave for a long time. When he finally stood up, his mother took him in her arms and that was when he finally let go. All the tears that he had kept bottled inside over the past thirty-five hours came flowing.

Chapter 21

Flashback to a Year Now Gone

A couple of days later, he borrowed Rituraj's laptop and went to the church to see Aastha's message. He laid a rose on her grave and then sat on the same bench where they had once sat.

He opened her email account. There was a mail from her to herself: 'My Second Last Secret'. It was dated a couple of days before their wedding.

He clicked on it. There was a video attached that took a while to download.

With almost-trembling fingers, he clicked on the play button.

There she was again in her room, smiling at him! He went into a rapture for a brief moment before she started speaking.

'Hi, my love. I hope you're doing well, and more importantly, I hope that when you see this, it's not because something's gone wrong between us...'

She took a long pause, searching for the right words she thought she already had.

'... Memory can be a tricky thing. You can forget—deliberately blank out—things you don't want to remember. And you can—"mis-remember" things the way you want to... I need to tell you the truth. I've been wanting to do this for a long time... But first, please understand that the reason I haven't told you the truth is that I fell in love with you—much against my best efforts. Telling the truth would most probably have meant losing you. And I said to myself—what the hell, I'm just here for a year or two at most, so why not be selfish these last few days.

'The truth is... I *was* there at the bus stop that morning. But I'm not the girl who smiled at you.'

Aastha paused here, allowing for the dramatic impact she knew her words would have on Joseph. And she hadn't been wrong. 'Dumbfounded' would be a sorely inadequate term for his feelings at that moment.

'I saw everything happen. I was there when the milkman's bike tore your pants. I saw you stapling them up. But I wasn't across the street. I was on the same side, *behind* you.'

Joseph felt his feet go cold, and then the iciness crawled up his spine.

'You never saw me... The girl you smiled at, who you think was your soulmate, wasn't me.

'It was Nadia.'

The drop in temperature had turned into a ferris-wheel and Joseph, for only the second time in his life, realised what it was like to be told something so astounding that it made him dizzy. It took him a few seconds to recover and refocus his attention on Aastha.

'Is it a coincidence that your soulmate should turn out to be my very own best friend? Not really, because we were always together. We were classmates in school and college, and we learnt singing together. If you had just looked around and seen where we were going while you were stapling your pants, you'd have found her much sooner... because you'd have seen where we entered—Guwahati Music College.'

Of course! That day was a Sunday! Singing lessons day. If Joseph had made enquiries at the Guwahati Music College about students in 2002, he might have very well have been kicked out of the place, but he might also have found a sympathetic ear who could have told him that there were seven girls in that batch, and just two of them fit his description. Instead, he had embarked on a wild-goose chase of over four hundred grey skirts.

'Here's another thing: Nadia remembers your pants ripping and all, but she doesn't remember smiling at you. She might have been, but it's also likely that she was in fact smiling at me, standing behind you.'

Joseph was lucky that he was sitting, or else he might well have rocked back on his heels and fallen into the nearest drain, because that was exactly where his soulmates theory seemed to be headed for. If Nadia hadn't been smiling at him at all, but at Aastha, then his whole notion of a once-in-a-lifetime romantic encounter went poof and turned into a silly little everyday misunderstanding instead. And if she *had* been smiling at him, how could it have been significant if she couldn't even remember that supposedly divine moment now?

'When I found out about your search and heard the song, I knew immediately that you were talking about Nadia. But she already had a boyfriend, so I thought I'd just meet this idiotically romantic guy—you. I thought I'd check you out and see if you were a good guy and worthy of my best friend.

'Everything I did from then on was totally stupid— all those tasks... I didn't want to fall in love with you, but—maybe I knew I would. Like I said—memory plays tricks on you.'

Aastha sighed, then said, 'I'm sorry for keeping you away from your true dream girl... but I'm not sorry for all the lovely times we've had together.'

'I'm not sorry either, sweetheart,' whispered Joseph.

'I've sent Nadia a video too, telling her everything. I'm not sure how she'll react, and I don't know whether after all this you guys will get together, but I think it'd be wonderful if you did. You'll get along really well. She's just like me, except that I think she's much wilder in bed,' said Aastha with a wink and a giggle, and Joseph couldn't help a smile himself.

'So there's the truth. The rest is up to you guys… Take your time, but do call her. I'll be happy if you spend this life with her. But remember, I'm advance-booking you for the next life… Well, bye then, darling. I'll always love you.'

'I'll always love you too, my darling,' said Joseph. The video ended. Joseph looked at the solitary rose on Aastha's grave.

Chapter 22

Four Months Later

Sitting on his parked bike, Joseph looked up at the signboard—'Guwahati Music College'—shook his head, and smiled in disbelief. His phone buzzed.

'Hi… You've arrived?… Outside your music college… Oh there you are.'

He waved at Nadia, who was standing across the street, having just got off a bus. She waved back and started crossing.

Joseph looked around. No milkboy this time.

Nadia reached him without incident.

'Hi,' she said.

'Hi.'

They smiled and shook hands.

'Are we meeting here by coincidence or by design?' she asked.

'Convenience. Easily identifiable landmark.'

'The college?'

'Yup... Have you had lunch?'
'Brunch actually. Feeling slightly hungry now.'
'What would you like?'
'I haven't had pork momos in a long time.'
'Let's go to Shikha restaurant, then.'

She climbed on the bike and they headed for the little fast-food restaurant opposite Guwahati Commerce College.

'So when d'you wanna move to Bombay?' said Nadia when their momos arrived.

'In a couple of months, I suppose.'

'I need a flatmate.'

'Great. I was hoping so. But isn't it difficult for unmarried boys and girls to get a place?'

'We'll tell them we're brother-sister.'

'No one'll believe us.'

'We'll say you were adopted, or that I'm the padosi ki aulad.'

westland
23/4/11